DEADLY COOL

DEADLY

COOL

GEMMA HALLIDAY

An Imprint of HarperCollinsPublishers

HarperTeen is an imprint of HarperCollins Publishers.

Deadly Cool
Copyright © 2011 by Gemma Halliday
All rights reserved. Printed in the United States of America.
No part of this book may be used or reproduced in any manner
whatsoever without written permission except in the case of brief
quotations embodied in critical articles and reviews. For information address HarperCollins Children's Books, a division of
HarperCollins Publishers, 10 East 53rd Street, New York, NY 10022.
www.epicreads.com

Library of Congress Cataloging-in-Publication Data
Halliday, Gemma.
Deadly cool / Gemma Halliday. — 1st ed.
    p. cm.
Summary: When sixteen-year-old Hartley Featherstone finds out that
her boyfriend is cheating on her, she goes to his house to confront him
and suddenly finds herself embroiled in a murder mystery.
ISBN 978-0-06-200331-7 (pbk. bdg.)
[1. Mystery and detective stories. 2. High schools—Fiction.
3. Schools—Fiction.] I. Title.
PZ7.H15449De 2011   2011010036
[Fic]—dc22   CIP
                                                              AC

Typography by Torborg Davern
11 12 13 14 15   CG/BV   10 9 8 7 6 5 4 3 2 1
❖
First Edition

FOR MY MOM,
WHOSE TOFU RICE CASSEROLE
IS THE MOST COMFORTING FOOD
ON THE PLANET

ACKNOWLEDGMENTS

WHILE WRITING IS USUALLY A VERY SOLITARY JOB, IT TAKES a village to turn one writer's thoughts into an actual book. So I have to acknowledge my very cool village, starting with the amazingly perky-and-helpful-at-crazy-early-hours-in-the-morning crew at the Blossom Hill Starbucks for all their support, friendly faces, and excellent lattes (the fuel that drove this book). Michelle, Holly, Angie, Daina, Dave, Kevin, Danielle, Angela, and Mike, you guys rock!

A great big thanks to Nicky, my teen linguistics expert, who has saved me from looking totally lame more than once.

Thanks to the Romance Divas for always having my back and being my BFFs 4ever.

And finally a big, heartfelt thanks to my Agent Awesome, Holly Root; my incredible editor, Erica Sussman, and her fabulous assistant, Tyler Infinger. Thanks for helping me bring Hartley and her world to life!

"We're censoring now?"

"Kyle says I have a mouth like a trucker."

"You do have a mouth like a trucker. It's one of the things I love best about you."

"Kyle says it's not very feminine."

I rolled my eyes toward the ceiling. "Yeah, I'd be taking femininity tips from a guy who lives in his football jersey."

Sam put her hands on her hips and threw me a pointed look. "Yeah? Well, at least *my* boyfriend's not effing the president of the Chastity Club."

I looked down at the Trojan wrapper in my hand. She had a point.

"God, this cannot be happening," I moaned.

Which is exactly what I'd been saying ever since Ashley Stannic texted me during first period English that someone had seen my boyfriend, Josh DuPont, feeling up Courtney Cline after cross-country practice yesterday. At first, I'd dismissed it. Because (A) Courtney Cline was the staying-a-virgin queen, putting up Earn Your Right to Wear White! posters all over the cafeteria and even urging students to sign an abstinence pledge the first day of school, and (B) Josh and I had been dating for, like, ever. Our relationship had even survived going long distance for two whole months this summer—one while I went to Ohio to visit my grandma Mimi and another when Josh went to soccer camp in Sacramento. Each one had felt like an eternity, but

ONE

THERE ARE THREE THINGS YOU NEVER WANT TO FIND in your boyfriend's locker: a sweaty jockstrap, a D minus on last week's history test, and an empty condom wrapper.

Lucky me, I'd hit the trifecta.

I pushed past the near-failing grade and underwear, honing in on the ripped foil packet. I grasped it between my thumb and forefinger, actually feeling my jaw drop open like some cartoon character as I leaned against the locker for support.

"No way," my best friend, Sam, said as she peered over my shoulder. "Hartley, is that . . . ?"

"I think so," I croaked out.

"Holy effing crap, that sucks!"

I turned to her. "Effing?"

Sam shrugged. "What?"

once he got home again, we spent the entire week before school started glued to each other's sides, only letting go when one of us had to sleep or pee. We were solid. I knew there was no way he would step out on me. Ashley *must* have been mistaken.

Only, by second period both Jessica Hanson and Chris Fret were mistaken, too, texting me to ask if the rumors of Josh hitting second base with Courtney were true. By lunch, half the school was mistaken, and I was the recipient of sidelong glances and barely concealed snickers over trays of pizza sticks and applesauce.

And I was questioning that solidity.

So, I did what any good girlfriend would do. I broke into Josh's locker. Would the more mature thing have been to confront him directly with the rumors? Possibly. Would it have been as effective?

I looked at the shiny gold-foil square in my hand.

Doubtful.

No matter how much I may love—scratch that, *loved*, past tense—Josh, I was no dummy. Everyone knows the Y chromosome carries with it the instinctive urge to lie under pressure.

Which, incidentally, was what Josh was going to be under when I found him. Serious pressure.

On his larynx.

I balled the wrapper in my fist. "Where is he?" I

demanded of the world at large. "Where is that cheating piece of—"

But I didn't get any further. The bell sounded above me, echoing off the halls of Herbert Hoover High. Immediately conversations around us stopped, lockers slammed shut, and hundreds of shoes squeaked against the overwaxed floors as people scattered to fifth period.

"Look, maybe there's a good reason for it being there," Sam offered, shrugging her backpack onto her shoulder.

"Such as?" I shoved the wrapper into my plaid book bag, slammed Josh's locker shut, and followed Sam down the hall.

"Well, maybe it's for sex ed class?"

"I don't know about you, but the last time I had sex ed was in eighth grade."

"Good point. Okay, maybe it's for some science project about, um, reproduction?"

"You're totally grasping."

"Fine. But maybe it's just one he used with you, and the wrapper got stuck in his backpack or something. That could happen, right?"

I bit my lip. No, it couldn't. Because my dirty little secret that I couldn't even share with my best friend? Unlike the president of the Chastity Club, I was an actual virgin.

Okay, I hadn't signed any pledge or made any promises to save myself for some hyped up Mr. Right to propose.

It just . . . well . . . it hadn't really happened for me yet. I'd tried. Once. During freshman year when it seemed like everyone was doing it, and I thought I was destined to be the only virgin left in the entire Silicon Valley. I'd been going out with Cole Perkins for a couple months at the time, so when he wanted me to come over to his place one Friday after water polo practice, I agreed.

His room had smelled like stale pizza, gym socks, and the Glade air freshener his mom used. He'd docked his iPod and played some horrible list of Christina Aguilera songs that I guess were supposed to put me in the mood but really just made me question what I was doing getting naked with a guy who downloaded Christina Aguilera songs. Cole swore he'd done this lots of times before, but I'd bet money that was his Y chromosome talking because it had been awkward, kinda painful, and in the end he'd squirted all over his bedsheets before we could even really do it.

After that one experience, I figured I probably wasn't missing out on much after all and gave up on the idea.

Until Josh. I'd always assumed that I'd do it someday with Josh. You know, when the timing was right.

Apparently the timing had been right with Courtney Cline first.

"Look, we'll track him down after school," Sam promised, pausing outside her lit class. "Don't worry, Hart. I'm sure this is all some big misunderstanding."

She gave my arm a quick squeeze before disappearing into the classroom. I stared after her, vaguely hearing the tardy bell fill the hallway with its ugly warning.

Right. Misunderstanding.

Josh better pray that's all this was. Otherwise, I was gonna *effing* kill him.

TWO

THE FIRST THING I DID WHEN I GOT TO CHEM (ONLY two minutes late) was text Josh. If he had a good explanation, now would be an excellent time to hear it.

need 2 talk asap.

I set my cell to vibrate and shoved it in the pocket of my jeans. Then, reluctantly, I opened my chem book, trying to follow along with the class while my entire being was focused on waiting for that telltale vibration of Josh's response.

One explanation of ionic versus covalent chemical bonding later, my phone still hadn't buzzed. As Mrs. Perry turned her back to write our homework assignment on the whiteboard, I pulled it out and tried again.

911 call when u get this.

Then I tucked it away again, pretending to care about

atoms swapping electrons.

But by the end of the class my phone was still conspicuously silent. I tried to catch a glimpse of Josh in the hallway as we scrambled for last period, but considering he had history in the east wing and I had trig in the west wing, it was a lost cause.

I sent three more texts during math, trying to concentrate on functions of acute angles, but completely distracted by the lack of activity coming from my pocket. With each second that ticked by, I could feel the possibility of this being just some stupid misunderstanding becoming slimmer and slimmer, until by the end of the period, it began to resemble an Olsen twin. On crack. After a colon cleanse.

So, as soon as the bell rang and the halls filled with people making their mad dash for freedom, I called Sam and told her to meet me on the field where the cross-country team practiced.

By the time I'd navigated the mass exodus, Sam was already there, watching the team stretch before their first run. I scanned the group of guys in orange and black HHH Wildcats jerseys for any sign of Josh's blond hair. Usually he stood out in a crowd—tall and lean, a shaggy-chic haircut, and the bluest eyes I'd ever seen. Think Zac Efron. But blond. And hotter. There was something about his smile—kinda lopsided with dimples—that drew both guys and girls into his circle like little mosquitoes buzzing toward a bright, shiny bug zapper. For better or worse, no one could resist Josh DuPont.

But, today, there was no sign of him.

Undeterred, I stalked up to a short guy with wiry black hair at the head of the track who was struggling to touch his toes. "Hey, Cody."

Cody Banks looked up, sweat already collecting on his wide brow. "Hey, Hartley. 'Sup." He nodded at Sam.

"'Sup."

Sam nodded back.

"Where's Josh?" I asked.

Cody shrugged. "Dunno."

"He's not at practice?"

He shook his head. "Nope. He hung out for a few minutes, but then he said he wasn't feelin' well. Maybe he went home."

Coward. If Josh thought he wasn't feeling well now, just wait till I got my hands on him . . .

"So," Cody said, leaning in closer, "is it true? About Josh and Courtney?"

I shot him a look that clearly said if he valued his life, he wouldn't go there.

"She found a condom wrapper," Sam supplied instead. "But we're pretty sure it's for a science project."

Cody shook his head. "Dude. Sucks."

"I know, right?" Sam said.

I ignored them, squinting into the sun as I swept my gaze across the field toward the bleachers where the Color Guard was practicing, twirling their oversize flags in the afternoon breeze like fluttering batons. While it wasn't a total given that all members of the Color Guard also belonged to the Chastity Club, twirling flags was considered one of the most wholesome activities on campus, meaning the ratio of Chastity girls in Color Guard was something like that of Mormons in Utah. I scanned the line of girls in short-skirted little uniforms. One perky brunette bob was conspicuously missing from the formation.

Courtney's.

I turned to my friend. "Sam, think you could borrow your brother's car?"

"Probably." She paused. "Why?"

"Because if I find Courtney Cline at Josh's and kill them both, I'm going to need a quick getaway."

Sam bit her lip, her eyebrows doing a concerned pucker on my behalf. But, good friend that she was, she finally said, "Okay, but we need to think of a convincing alibi on the way."

Half an hour later we were rolling down Blossom Hill Road in her brother Kevin's 1986 Volvo sedan with Live Green! bumper stickers plastered all over the back. Much to their parents' dismay, Sam's brother had dropped out of college and joined Greenpeace last year instead of graduating from Stanford like his father had. And *his* father had. And *his* father had. It was a Kramer family tradition that had ended painfully when her mom had found Kevin not in the undergrad Business Law class he was supposed to be taking, but outside the Whole Foods with a clipboard in hand, urging shoppers to sign a petition to decrease urbanization in the swamps of the black-spotted river toad. While her parents freaked, Sam had been cool with her brother either way—Stanford alum or hippie frog lover. That was, until her parents made it clear she was now their sole hope of having a child graduate from college, go on to be a celebrated surgeon, and make enough to support them in a fancy retirement village in their old age. Needless to say, Sam's trig grades had become the sole topic of conversation around the Kramer family dinner table.

Lucky for us, Sam's parents were still both at work, and Kevin had traded us his keys in exchange for a promise to use recycled paper for our homework that night.

Unluckily, a 1986 Volvo sedan crawls only slightly faster than a Segway.

"Can't you make this thing move?" I asked, watching an old lady in a giant Buick pass us.

"Sorry. Kevin put an SVO conversion on the engine, and it's kinda slow."

I cocked my head. "SVO?"

Sam nodded. "Straight vegetable oil. It burns cleaner than traditional fuel. Basically just dump a bunch of cooking oil in the tank, and we're good to go."

"Seriously?" No wonder Granny was passing us.

"Yep. Kevin goes around to all the fast-food restaurants to collect their used oil once a week."

"Gross."

"I know. But it'll get us there," Sam promised. "Which leads me to ask . . . what exactly are you going to *do* when we get there?"

I thought about it. "Rip Josh's nuggets off and feed them to his hamster?"

Sam nodded. "Creative." Then she turned to me as she slowed for a stop sign. "But seriously. What are you going to say?"

I sighed, leaned my head back on the seat, and closed my eyes. "I don't know."

Which, I realized, was the truth. I had no idea what I was supposed to say in a situation like this. I knew I was supposed to be angry at him. And I was. That feeding-his-family-jewels-to-the-hamster thing might have been a joke, but it wasn't too far off the mark. Every time I thought of that condom wrapper burning a hole through my book bag, I wanted to hit something.

Hard.

Preferably his face.

But, as much as I hated to admit it, part of me kinda didn't want to hate him. Kinda didn't want to break up with him even though that seemed like the logical next step. What I really wanted was to go back to yesterday when everything was fine, I had a great boyfriend, and Courtney Cline knew how to keep her legs together.

Sam rounded the corner onto Beacon and pulled our clean-burning machine to a stop with a quick cough of relief from the engine. Which was starting to smell like French fries.

Beacon was like any other street in suburban Silicon Valley: California ranch-style homes built one right next to the other, squares of lawn out front with mature trees acting as a buffer between the street, minivans and SUVs with those little stick figure families in the back windows resting in every drive. By seven, the neighborhood would be filled with the scents of meat loaf and the sounds of *Jeopardy*. Currently, the only sign of life was a guy three doors down, taking photos of an old Camaro with a dented bumper in his driveway.

And Josh's Jeep Wrangler parked in front of the curb.

I took a deep breath. God, what *was* I going to say to him? What was he going to say to me? Would he try to deny it? Lie his way out of it? Maybe he'd confess and beg for forgiveness, promise he'd never touch another girl again as long as he lived. Would I believe him?

"So . . . you going in?" Sam asked from the driver's seat.

I nodded. "Uh-huh." But for some reason, my butt stayed firmly glued to my seat.

"Sometime soon?"

"Sure."

"Before we graduate?"

"Maybe."

"You scared?"

"Totally."

"Do you want me to come with you?"

I nodded. "Would you?"

Sam grinned. "Hey, I'm already driving the getaway car. I might as well be a full-blown accomplice. Let's go." She hopped out of the car, forcing me to do the same, and grabbed my hand as we crossed the street and made our way up the walkway to Josh's front door. A little stone goose dressed in a rain slicker sat on the porch, two pairs of muddy gardening Crocs beside it. On the door hung a wreath of dried flowers with a little Welcome sign in the center.

"What if his mom answers?" Sam asked, staring at the goose as if it might come to life and begin pecking her kneecaps.

I shook my head. "His parents are on some cruise to Alaska. Anniversary." Which yesterday had meant we could make out all we wanted on his living room couch with no one to bother us. Today . . . the thought of my tongue touching any tongue that had touched Courtney Cline's tongue sent a wave of nausea running through me.

I sucked in a breath of courage, squeezed Sam's hand for support, and rang the bell before I could change my mind. Muted chimes echoed on the other side of the door, and I strained to hear the sound of footsteps approaching. Silence greeted us instead, so I hit the bell again, feeling Sam shift nervously from foot to foot beside me.

No answer.

I gave up on the bell, pounding a fist on the front door just below the Welcome sign. "We know you're in there, Josh! Open up!"

I thought I heard movement inside, but after waiting a full minute we were still standing on the porch like idiots. I grabbed the door handle and jiggled it. Locked. Great.

"Maybe he's not here." Sam peered in the front window, craning her head to see around the oversize sofa and oak entertainment center.

"His car is here."

"Maybe he's just not answering? Maybe he figures if he doesn't answer the door, you can't break up with him."

I narrowed my eyes, my anxiety converting to determination. "Let's go around back."

I crossed the lawn to the wooden side gate, reaching

around the top, and popping the latch.

"Back door?" Sam asked, struggling to keep up with my purposeful march.

I nodded, reaching the sliding glass doors that led into Josh's family room. Only, as I tugged on the handle, it became clear those were locked, too.

"Looks like we're not getting in," Sam said.

I surveyed the backyard. Thick green grass covered the lawn, and fruit trees stood along the fence shielding the yard for privacy. To the right was a covered patio with a barbecue large enough to roast a small elephant. To the left, a portable storage shed sat flush against the stuccoed wall of the house. I looked up. The shed's roof ended only a few feet shy of the second story.

Just under Josh's bedroom window.

Sam followed my gaze. Then bugged her eyes at me. "You have got to be kidding me."

"If we can get on the roof, it'll be easy to climb in the window."

"What are you, ten? Who climbs on roofs?"

I turned on her. "Look, I've got two choices here, Sam. I can either climb onto the shed, go in the window, and make Josh explain why a condom wrapper was in his locker, or I can go home, text him twenty more times, and wait by the phone like some pathetic sap while I imagine him swapping God knows what bodily fluids with Courtney Cline."

Sam bit the inside of her cheek, her gaze going to the roof again. "Effing hell. I hate heights."

"Don't worry, it's not that high," I assured her. Even though I wasn't totally keen on high places myself. While mandatory PE and the occasional trip to the gym kept me in single digit sizes, I wasn't exactly what you'd call athletic. And that shed looked like it was made out of recycled cans.

But no way was I playing the text-waiting game any longer.

I cracked my knuckles, then dug the toes of my Skechers into the corrugated metal side of the shed, grasping at the edge of the roof with my fingertips. "Give me a boost," I instructed Sam.

A second later I felt her hands on the seat of my jeans, shoving me upward with a grunt.

"One crack about the size of my butt, and I'll disown you," I warned, my triceps straining as my feet slipped, doing a jogging-in-the-air thing. Finally they found their grip again, scrambling up the side as I hoisted myself onto the roof belly first.

The shed gave a low groan under my weight, and I lay perfectly still, half expecting the entire thing to collapse under me.

It didn't. Which I took as a good sign.

I scrambled to my hands and knees, leaning down to help Sam. She kicked off her flip-flops to get better traction, threw them to me first, then grabbed my hand and crawled up the side of the shed to join me.

Again the structure groaned as Sam flopped onto the roof beside me, both of us pausing to catch our breath.

"Now what?" she asked, eyeing Josh's bedroom window as she slipped her shoes back on.

I stood on tiptoe, trying to get a good look inside. The curtains were shut, so I couldn't make out much. Just a flash of color between the panels that could have been someone's shoulder or just as easily a lampshade.

"I'm going in," I decided.

"Are you sure this is a good idea?" Sam hedged.

No, I wasn't. But since it was the only idea I had, I slipped my fingers between the frame and the windowsill, slowly lifting the window until I had a good three feet of clearance. I paused, listening for any sounds from within.

Nothing.

I took a deep breath, parted the curtains, hoisted myself up and over the sill, and then lowered myself into Josh's room, Sam a step behind me.

Most of the room was in shadow, the only light source the window we'd just crawled through. My eyes glanced over Josh's bed, unmade, covered in the same solar-system-themed sheets he'd had since fifth grade. Beside it sat his desk, with his laptop and a collection of textbooks strewn on top. A shelf above held his sports trophies—cross-country, baseball, soccer. Lots of little chrome guys holding balls, contorted in uncomfortable positions. On the opposite side of the room was a wooden dresser and a pile of dirty clothes that I blamed for the slightly sour smell in the room. And next to that was Josh's closet.

Where my eyes froze.

In the crack between the wall and closet door, the purple, shimmery, spandex fabric of an HHH Color Guard uniform stared back at me.

Gotcha.

I poked Sam in the arm, gesturing to the closet. Her eyes went big as she mouthed the words, "Oh my God!"

I slowly tiptoed toward the closet, sure the sound of my heart pounding was loud enough for Sam to hear. I reached a hand out and quickly slid the door back . . .

To reveal Courtney Cline, cowering on the floor of my boyfriend's closet.

"I knew it!" I shouted.

Only Courtney didn't move. Her head was bent downward, her hair covering her face as if pretending she couldn't see me would make her invisible, too.

"I see you, Courtney. Get up," I commanded, towering over her, hands on hips in what I hoped was a very intimidating pose.

Only she still didn't move.

Okay, now she was *really* starting to piss me off.

"Hart—" Sam started.

But I held up a hand to stop her. Whatever she had to say could wait. At the sight of Miss Chastity, the fear that had been growing in my gut all day was suddenly confirmed in the flesh. And the resulting adrenaline pumping through my system was too good to waste. Courtney and I were going to have this out here and now.

"I said get up!" I repeated, then punctuated my command by grabbing her scrawny arm and yanking her forward.

But as Courtney's head dropped back like a rag doll's, I realized there was no way she was getting up. Her hair fell away to reveal her porcelain pale face. Her big, blue eyes were open, staring straight ahead. Her mouth was fixed in a surprised little O. And the smooth, blemish-free skin of her long, dancer's neck was bruised purple beneath the cord of her white iPod earbuds, wrapped in a deadly stranglehold around her throat.

THREE

MY FAVORITE MOVIE OF ALL TIME IS *BORAT*. AND THE absolute best scene in the movie is when Borat catches his totally fat (we're talking his rolls have rolls) friend, Azamat, in a hotel room, defiling a picture of Borat's beloved Pamela Anderson. Borat freaks, charges at Azamat, and the two of them start wrestling, buck naked, throughout the entire hotel. The scene is hilarious. But two hairy, old, naked guys wrestling? The single most disgusting thing I have ever seen in my life.

Until now.

I dropped Courtney's arm as if it was on fire, quickly shaking my hands up and down to get rid of the dead person cooties. Then I screamed. Long, loud, until my throat hurt. I vaguely registered Sam doing the same thing, then shoving past me toward the hall. I followed her, the two of us screeching like banshees and running for the front door like Olympic sprinters.

"Ohmigod, ohmigod, ohmigod!" Sam chanted, as we pushed and shoved each other toward the stairs. We took them two at a time, half sliding, half falling down the last few in our mad dash for the door. Sam hit it first, fumbling with the lock before finally throwing it open and running down the front steps, arms flailing.

I collapsed onto the curb. My legs felt wobbly, my heart was pounding too fast, and my breath came out in irregular little chokes as I blinked at Josh's house, trying to process what we'd just seen.

"Shewasdeadright?" Sam said, her words slurring together with urgency. "I mean, really, really dead."

I nodded.

"Ohmigod, ohmigod!" Sam plunked down on the curb next to me. "We saw a dead body. A real dead body. You *touched* a dead body!"

My stomach clenched, and I wiped my palm against my thigh. "I think I'm gonna be sick."

"Josh has a dead body in his room. Ohmigod, your boyfriend cheated on you with a dead body!"

"Would you stop saying 'dead body'!" I shouted. "And I'm sure she was alive when . . . you know . . ." I wiped my palm on my jeans again.

"Ohmigod, what are we going to do?" Sam asked, her

voice rising into hysterics territory.

"What's going on?"

I whipped my head around to find Camaro Guy standing over us, camera dangling from his right hand.

I thought I vaguely recognized him from school, though he wasn't in any of my classes. His hair was dark, cropped close and a little spiky on top. He wore unrelieved black from head to toe—black pants, black T-shirt, jet-black hair—and I wasn't sure, but it looked like he was even wearing black eyeliner. The whole effect gave him a dark, dangerous vibe, intensified by the way he was towering over us.

"What's the screaming about?" he asked again, his gaze jumping from us, crumpled in a heap on the sidewalk, to Josh's front door.

I opened my mouth to speak, but only a strangled sort of cry in the back of my throat came out. I took a deep breath and tried again, this time finding my voice, albeit a shaky one. "In there," I said, pointing to the house. "Courtney."

The guy raised an eyebrow in my direction, clearly not getting it. "You two okay?"

I shook my head back and forth so violently that my hair whipped at my cheeks, stinging them. "No. Not okay. Dead. Courtney's dead."

This time both his eyebrows went north. "Dead?"

Beside me Sam nodded. "Upstairs. In the closet." She turned to me. "Hartley found her. She touched her."

I elbowed her in the ribs. Did she have to keep reminding me? My palm was getting raw from rubbing it against my thigh.

The guy in black looked from Sam to me, then at the house, no doubt trying to figure out if this was part of some elaborate joke at his expense. But the fact that neither of us could stop shaking must have convinced him, because he finally said, "Wait here," then walked up the front path to Josh's and disappeared inside.

Sam grabbed my hand. I squeezed back. And we waited in silence for him to come out.

Two minutes later, he did, his face a shade of pale that even a *Twilight* actor couldn't achieve.

"Give me your cell," he barked at me.

I complied, extracting it from my pocket. "Who are you calling?"

He gave me a hard look, his jaw clenched at a tight angle. Then he answered, "The police."

"Name?"

"Hartley Grace Featherstone.

"Age?"

"Sixteen."

"Address?"

"One seventeen Orange Grove, San José."

"School?"

"Herbert Hoover High. Um, Detective Raley?"

"Yes?"

"I think I need to throw up again."

The big, redheaded guy, whose suit looked like it had shrunk two sizes in the wash, took one giant step back as I shoved my head between my knees to keep the world from spinning.

As soon as the guy in black had called 911, the air seemed to fill with the sound of sirens. An ambulance was soon on the scene, paramedics rushing into Josh's house with first-aid kits. Once it became as obvious to them as it was to Sam and me that Courtney was beyond help, the uniformed police arrived. That's when the guy in black had quietly disappeared, leaving Sam and me to our own devices. Not surprising. From the look of Tall, Dark, and Dangerous I'd say he made a habit of avoiding authority like most people avoid Brussels sprouts.

Once the police had gotten a look at Josh's room, they'd called in Detective Raley from homicide, who had then sent for the guy from the crime scene unit (who, by the way, looked nothing like the hot guy on CBS). But it was when the black coroner's van finally arrived that I'd lost it and tossed my partially digested pizza sticks into Mrs. DuPont's azalea bushes. Up until then, it had all been sort of surreal, almost like watching a scene unfold on TV. The uniformed officers fending off a growing crowd of curious stay-at-home moms, CSU dusting the front door for fingerprints; and blue and red lights from the squad cars bathing the entire neighborhood in hues that were half dance club, half kindergartner coloring book.

But seeing the coroner wheel a gurney from the back of his van up the front walkway to Josh's house made me realize just how dead Courtney was and just what kind of trouble Sam and I were in.

"Doing okay?" Raley asked, laying a tentative hand on my back.

I took a few more deep breaths from the curb, inhaling the scents of rainwater, someone's nearby barbecue, and the rubber from my shoes. Then I lifted my head and slowly nodded. "I think so."

At which the detective looked immensely relieved. I'd venture to say vomiting teens hadn't been in his job description. He looked old enough to be someone's dad, but maybe not quite to grandpa stage yet. Red hair, round belly, lots of freckles, and a generous helping of wrinkles that said he was too tough for sunscreen.

"I just have a few more questions, then you can go home, okay?"

I nodded again. Then stole a glance across the street, where Sam was on her cell, talking faster than a chipmunk on Starbucks to her boyfriend about our gruesome discovery. Knowing Kyle, it would be all over school in a matter of minutes. I willed my queasy stomach not to think about it.

"You said your boyfriend lives here?"

"Yeah. Josh. Josh DuPont."

"And the victim . . ." He looked down, consulting his notes.

"Courtney," I supplied, finding myself feeling sorry for her despite all I'd learned that day.

"Right. Courtney Cline." He looked up, his heavily lined face puckering in concern. "What was she doing here?"

I bit the inside of my cheek. "Most likely effing my boyfriend."

"Effing?"

"It means—"

Raley held up a beefy hand. "Uh, I think I know what it means." His cheeks tinged red, but he cleared his throat and continued. "So, Courtney was 'seeing' your boyfriend?" he asked, doing air quotes around the substitute verb.

I nodded.

"And you came here to confront her?"

"Well, no. I mean, I came to confront Josh, really, but we found her instead."

"And things got out of hand?" he asked.

"Yeah. Wait—no!" I narrowed my eyes at him. "What do you mean, 'got out of hand'?"

He paused as if choosing his words very carefully. "Courtney was murdered, Hartley."

And while I knew it was pretty unlikely that Courtney had accidentally strangled herself with her iPod earbuds, hearing the words out loud sent my stomach lurching again.

"We did not kill her," I said. "We were just coming to talk to Josh. Only he chickened out and wasn't here."

"So, Josh knew you were coming to confront him?"

"That would be my guess."

"And he got here first?" he asked, gesturing to Josh's Jeep.

I shrugged. "Looks like it."

"And made sure Courtney would keep his secret."

"What? No. You think Josh . . . ? No. No way."

"No?"

I shook my head again. "There is no way Josh could have done this."

"You're sure?"

"Positive. I know Josh."

"You didn't know he was sleeping with someone else."

I bit my lip. Good point. "Look, he may not be perfect"—understatement alert—"but I know Josh isn't a killer."

"Okay," Raley said, holding up his hands in a surrender gesture. "Let's switch gears for a minute, then. Courtney. Tell me how you found her?"

"In the closet." I swallowed, wiping my palm against the side of my jeans again as I relived the scene. I had a bad feeling I was never going to be able to cleanse my brain of those images.

"How did you get in the house?"

"What?" I asked, snapping back to the present.

"You said the front door was locked, correct? So how did you get in the house?"

"Oh. Right . . ." Compared to killing someone, I was pretty sure sneaking in an upstairs window was small potatoes. But, seeing as I was already starting to feel like a suspect, I didn't want to chance it. "Uh, we sorta went around back."

"Sorta?"

"Yeah. Sorta."

"Hartley," he said, leaning in close, his voice lowering an octave into that friendly slash fatherly thing that the cops on *Law & Order* did right before they arrested someone, "the CSU team is going over the entire house right now. Fingerprints, footprints, hair, clothing fibers. Why don't you make things easy on yourself and tell me the truth?"

Why was it when someone told you to make things

easier on yourself it was never by doing something easy?

"We went around back," I repeated.

"And?" he prodded.

"Do you really need all the details?"

He nodded. "Yeah, I kind of do."

"Fine." I sighed, giving in. "We hopped onto the top of the storage shed and climbed in Josh's window."

He frowned. "You know that breaking into someone else's house is illegal?"

"Not as illegal as killing someone. Which," I said, making the point again, "we didn't do."

"All right, all right. I'll let it go for now."

I put a hand to my head where a migraine was brewing. "So, can I go home now?"

"I'll have an officer drive you home in a minute. I just have one more question."

I nodded. "Hit me."

"Where is Josh DuPont?"

I bit my lip. Good one.

And I wished to God I had an answer.

When the police finally let Sam and me go, they took down our personal information, said they'd be in touch with our parents (joy), and told us both to stick around town. Which was so clichéd I almost laughed out loud. A sure sign I was going into some sort of shock because there was clearly nothing funny about this situation. Courtney was dead, I was a material witness, and Josh was MIA.

While Raley assured me that all the questions he'd asked were routine, the way he kept frowning every time I mentioned Josh didn't fill me with a whole lot of confidence that he wasn't writing the word "suspect" in big, bold letters next to his name. Courtney was found in his house; he was missing; and, as the detective had pointed out, he had a crap-ton of motive.

I closed my eyes, trying not to think about that as a uniformed officer drove me home. Instead, I texted Josh again from the backseat of the squad car.

where the hell r u?!!

By the time the officer dropped me off at home, it was all I could do to drag myself through the door, drop my book bag on the sofa, and raid the back of the freezer for a pint of Cherry Garcia from my hidden ice cream stash. I grabbed a spoon and dug in, leaning against the kitchen counter. I was three bites closer to calm when Mom walked in, Nikes on her feet and a basket of laundry under her arm.

"Geez, Hartley, get a bowl, would you?" she said, grabbing one from the cupboard above the sink.

I refrained from pointing out that I intended to eat the entire carton and instead scooped what was left into the dish.

"I've got yoga in twenty," Mom said as she trailed into the laundry room. "So you're on your own for dinner. And ice cream does not count. There's leftover rice pizza in the fridge."

I wrinkled my nose. Mom didn't eat gluten, hence the rice-crust pizza. She also didn't eat dairy. Or processed foods. Or meat. Which basically left her existing on exercise.

"Fine," I answered, scooping another mouthful of B & J's onto my tongue.

"How was your day?" she asked, grabbing a soy protein shake from the fridge.

Bad. Awful. Deadly.

But after enduring Detective Raley's interrogation, I couldn't face another one from Mom. At least not until I'd had time to put together an edited-for-parents version. So, instead, I went with the standard, "Fine."

"Great. Listen, I'm meeting some of the girls for coffee after yoga, so I'll be late. Don't wait up. Oh," she added, grabbing her keys from the hook by the garage door, "and get cracking on your homework. Don't save it all for the last minute again this week, huh?"

"On it," I lied as she disappeared out the door. A beat later I heard her minivan start up and the garage door rumble closed behind her.

Generally, I'm a pretty honest person. And my 3.5 GPA

attests to the fact that, despite my tendency to procrastinate, I almost always get my homework done on time. But tonight I just didn't have it in me.

So I ignored Mom's decree about ice cream not constituting a complete meal and trudged up the stairs to my bedroom, flopping spread-eagled on my patchwork quilt as I tried to block out the gruesome slide show of my day.

I shut my eyes, took a few deep, cleansing breaths . . . then felt my cell buzz to life in my jeans.

Josh.

I grabbed for it, catching a nail on the edge of my pocket in my clumsy haste before flipping it open.

A number that was clearly not Josh's lit up the display. Crap. I swallowed down the surge of disappointment as I read the text from Ashley Stannic.

is it true? cc dead?

I bit my lip. Courtney's entire life had just been reduced to one line of text. Granted, I hadn't been the president of her fan club, but I hadn't actually wanted to see her dead. (Maybe just maimed a little . . .)

I flipped the phone shut, dropping it on the quilt beside me, leaving Ashley to get her gossip elsewhere.

Two minutes later, my phone buzzed to life again. I looked at the readout. Jessica Hanson.

OMG! cc dead?

I deleted the message, slowly setting my cell down

again. Or trying to. It buzzed in my hand before I could even let go.

ding dong the bitch is dead!

I quickly flipped it shut, a sick feeling churning in the pit of my stomach, warning of a repeat appearance by my Cherry Garcia.

A second later it buzzed again.

I immediately hit the power button without even checking the readout, then threw the offending device into my book bag as if it was a time bomb ready to go off.

I lay back on the bed, willing Ben & Jerry to stay put. Eventually I think I fell asleep. Because the next thing I knew, I was back in Josh's bedroom. It was dark; I could just make out shadows, flashes of color in the moonlight. And then I saw her: Courtney Cline, still dressed in her purple Color Guard uniform. But she wasn't slumped in the closet anymore. She was standing next to it. Walking toward me, her arms stretched in front of her like some sort of zombie. She was coming after me, I could feel it. I turned toward the door, but it was like my feet were stuck in molasses. I tried to call out for help, but I couldn't make my voice work. I tried harder to run, pumping my arms with all my might, willing my feet to move. But she was gaining on me, the Courtney zombie with the grotesque earbuds wrapped tightly around her neck. She was almost on top of me.

And then I tripped, falling to the floor. I felt her hovering over me, her shadow blocking out the last of the moonlight. I turned to face her. She reached out a hand and . . .

Fingers squeezed my shoulder. I screamed, bolting upright in bed. Sweat trickled down the small of my back, my breath coming out in ragged pants as I focused through the darkness at the figure in front of me.

Tall, lean, shaggy hair.

Josh.

I leaned over and turned on my bedside lamp, blinking against the sudden onslaught of light as I took him in.

"Holy effing crap, Josh. You scared me half to death."

"Effing?"

"We're censoring now," I explained.

"Oh. Sorry," he whispered. "I didn't mean to scare you." He sat down on the bed beside me.

Close beside me. So close I could smell his Axe body wash. Subtle and woodsy. I'd always loved the way it lingered after he'd been in my room. In spite of all that had happened, I inhaled deeply, something in my chest fluttering at the familiar scent.

"Hey, baby," he said, leaning in. I watched his lips move toward mine, his scent swirling in my nostrils.

I took a deep breath.

Then shoved him hard.

"What the hell, Hart!" Josh's head snapped back as he fell off the bed, landing in a heap on the floor.

But I wasn't done with him.

"You creep!" I threw my pillow at him. "You jerk!" I joined him on the floor and swatted him in the stomach. "You absolute effing rat turd!" I rained a hail of blows on his chest, channeling all the hours I'd ever spent Wii boxing, until he finally caught both my wrists in his hands.

"Hart, baby, calm down."

"You ever call me 'baby' again, and I swear your hamster will be using your nuggets as chew toys."

I'm not sure he totally believed the threat, but he was smart enough to let my hands go. He scooted backward on the carpet, putting some distance between us.

"How did you even get in here?" I asked, my eyes going to my bedroom door, trying to get my heart rate back under control.

"Window." He gestured at my curtains, fluttering in the breeze.

Did no one use the door?

"I couldn't take the chance of anyone seeing me," he explained.

As I tried to catch my breath, I took a good look at Josh. He looked awful—pale, tired, with dark, defeated circles under his eyes and lines of worry etched over his eyebrows. Despite the anger coursing through me, I had to fight the urge to reach out and hug him and tell him everything was going to be okay.

Then again, I had no idea if that was true.

"What happened to you today?" I asked.

Josh exhaled deeply and ran a hand through his perfectly mussed hair. "I don't know where to start."

"Start at the beginning. Where were you after school today?"

"I wasn't feeling well at practice—"

"Bull crap," I interrupted him.

He paused, clearly surprised. Then one corner of his mouth tilted up in his trademark smile. "All right, fine. I heard you were pissed. I was afraid you were going to do . . . well . . . what you just did. So I was avoiding you. Happy?"

Hardly. But I urged him on anyway. "Then what?"

"Well, I drove home, but I was restless. So I decided to go for a run. Next thing I know, I'm jogging back to my house and there's a ton of cop cars parked out on my front lawn. So I hightailed it out of there."

"Wait, why did you run? Didn't you want to see what was going on?"

Josh's eyes hit the floor. "I kinda had something on me."

I cocked my head. "'On you'? What kind of 'something'?"

"Something the cops wouldn't like."

I narrowed my eyes. "What. Kind. Of. Something."

"A fake ID, okay?" His cheeks tinged pink. "Last

Friday, Cody's older brother doctored a couple drivers' licenses for us so we could get into this over twenty-one show in Santa Cruz. I had the fake license in my pocket. I didn't want to get Cody's brother in trouble, so I figured I'd hang back till the cops left."

Why was it I'd never realized what a moron he was until now? "That was dumb."

He ignored me. "Anyway," he went on, "I went to Cody's house, and he told me what was up. That they'd found Courtney's body in my bedroom."

"Why didn't you go to the police then?"

Josh shook his head. "Someone killed her in my room. Look, the cops have already been at Cody's and Chris Fret's houses looking for me. And I'm pretty sure it's not to invite me to the policeman's ball."

"Josh, this is crazy," I said, hugging my knees to my chest. Even though a tiny part of me knew he was right. The way Raley had been questioning my movements, Josh clearly had some 'splainin' to do.

Josh leaned in closer so that his eyes caught the light from my single lamp, sparkling a blue so clear it was almost unreal. "I'm seventeen," he said. "Hart, I can be tried as an adult for this. This is serious."

"So what are you going to do?"

He looked down, picking at an invisible piece of lint on my carpet. "Lay low for a while. Hope someone finds the real killer before the cops track me down. Honestly, that's kind of why I'm here."

I narrowed my eyes at him. "What do you mean?"

He looked up, his gaze suddenly pleading. "Look, someone killed Courtney, and until the cops can nail that guy down, I'm going to be their number one suspect." He paused. "We need to find out who really killed Courtney."

"*We?*" I let out a short bark of a laugh. "You must be joking."

"Please, Hart, you're the only one I can trust."

"I'm sorry, trust is something I'm a little short on today." I crossed my arms over my chest.

But Josh leaned in and took one of my hands. I could feel my resolve weakening. I tried to stay strong, to remember that ball of rage I'd felt looking into his locker that afternoon. But his hands were warm. And after the day I'd had, they felt nice. Familiar. Comforting.

"Josh?" My voice came out barely a whisper.

He leaned in and I could smell the minty gum on his breath. "Yeah?"

"Did you do it?"

"What? No. God, no!" He pulled back, running a hand through his hair again, this time making it stand up in little tufts. "How can you even ask that, Hartley?"

I sat up on my knees. "Look me in the eyes, Josh." Which was a sign of just how desperate I was, because I'd never seen the look-me-in-the-eyes trick hold up in court.

Josh squared his jaw, his baby blue eyes meeting mine. I felt my chest flutter again but held tight to what little resolve I had left.

"Look me in the eyes and tell me you did not kill Courtney Cline."

Josh took a deep breath. "I swear on the cross-country championship trophy that I did not kill Courtney."

I rolled my eyes. Hardly sacred, but I let it go.

"Okay," I said, still holding his gaze. "Now swear that you didn't sleep with her."

"I . . ." He faltered, his eyes sliding to the floor before meeting mine again. "I didn't sleep with her."

I'd seen kindergartners lie better than that. I felt hope slowly shriveling into a sad little ball in my chest.

But.

He was easier to read than a Dick and Jane book. And when he'd said he didn't kill her, he'd been as straight as an arrow. He was no murderer.

"Please, Hart, you've got to believe me," he pleaded, taking my hand again.

I looked down at his thumb, aimlessly caressing the back of my hand. I told myself my decision had nothing to do with how good that felt as I gulped down what little bit of common sense I had left.

"Okay."

"Okay?" The glimmer of hope in Josh's eyes was enough to break my heart. I quickly looked away, telling myself I did not care what lit up his eyes anymore.

"I'll help you."

"Oh, Hart, you are the best—"

But I cut him off. "Let's be clear. I'm not doing this because I'm your girlfriend. We are so over that. Done. *Finito*. The end."

For a moment he looked like he might protest, but then his shoulders sagged in defeat. Apparently the day had taken the fight out of him as much as it had me.

"I'll help you," I said, softening my tone, "because I believe you."

He nodded, his eyes a little sad. "Thanks, Hartley. I appreciate it."

I pulled my hand away, shaking off the emotion I could feel backing up in my throat. "Look, the police will probably be watching your phone. How do I get hold of you?"

He reached into his back pocket and handed me a slip of paper with a name on it. HHHrunner94.

"What's this?" I asked.

"MySpace account. I created it at Cody's this afternoon."

I wrinkled my nose. "MySpace? No one is on there anymore."

"Exactly. What better place to hide out?"

Good point.

"Just message me there if you need me. I'll try to log in at least once a day, okay?"

I nodded.

"Thanks again, Hartley," he said, and leaned in as if to kiss me.

I quickly turned my face away.

He awkwardly stood up, moving to the window.

"Josh," I called, watching his long, lean frame climb over the sill.

He paused, turning so the shadows played across his features, softening them in the dim light. "Yeah?"

"Be careful."

He smiled. That million-dollar, charm-the-pants-off-any-girl, Josh DuPont smile.

And then he was gone.

I sank back on my pillows, alone again in the darkness, and stared at my ceiling.

What had I gotten myself into?

FOUR

WHEN I WAS TEN, MY PARENTS GOT DIVORCED. UP
until then I had lived in Los Angeles, where Dad wrote
sitcoms for a living and Mom stayed home and baked
gluten-free cookies. But single parenthood meant Mom
needed a job, so we had to move north to Silicon Valley,
where she could put her degree in programming to use
working for Google. The upside? Mom got to work from
home in the afternoons, meaning she was still free to bake
me after-school treats. The downside? I'd had to move to
suburbia.

The suburbs were a completely different experience for
a kid raised in the heart of the city like me. One I'd been
unprepared for. Little did I know that suburban kids had
mastered the art of the clique even better than their urban
counterparts.

On the very first day of fifth grade, the kids all looked at me like I was from another planet. Branded the new kid, there was no way I could have blended in. I'd been the three-headed monster walking down the halls of their familiar school, threatening all that was status quo.

Eventually I'd worn out my new-kid smell and convinced my classmates I could be as homogenous as they were, but I still remembered that as the most uncomfortably conspicuous I had ever felt.

It didn't hold a candle to today.

I bit my lip, feeling dozens of eyes on my back as I snaked down the halls of Herbert Hoover High Tuesday morning. I tried to ignore them, but they were everywhere, poised as if waiting for me to do something. Like return the seven hundred and fifty messages they'd collectively texted me last night. No joke. Seven hundred and freaking fifty. My mom was going to have a heart attack when she saw the Verizon bill.

Never in my life had the first bell sounded so sweet, sending the gawkers reluctantly scattering to their classes. I slipped into the back row of my lit class, immediately opening my book and pretending to read in order to avoid the stares of my classmates.

Only some didn't stop at staring.

I felt a pencil poke me in the back. I spun around to find Jessica Hanson leaning forward on her desk.

"Is it true," she whispered through her braces, "about Courtney?"

I bit my lip, feeling my breakfast latte churn in my stomach. And nodded.

"Woooooow," Jessica responded. Then leaned in again. "What did she look like? Was she, like, all messed up?" She scrunched her freckled nose up.

Luckily, the principal's voice over the loudspeaker saved me from replying.

"Good morning, students," he started. "I'm sorry to inform you that we've had some tragic news this morning."

There went that churning again.

"One of our beloved students," the principal went on, "Courtney Cline, has passed away."

I heard muffled gasps, and one of the Color Guard girls at the front of the class bowed her head and started sobbing. Several pairs of eyes glanced my way, a silent question hanging in the air—just how pissed at Courtney had I been yesterday?

I ducked my head, again feigning inordinate interest in Shakespeare's sonnets as the principal went on.

"We at Herbert Hoover High are both stunned and saddened by this untimely loss. We are providing a grief counselor to any student who may wish to take advantage of her services. You may meet with her in room twenty-five."

I managed to make it through English and PE, but by third period, I'd had enough of the stares, the whispers, people mouthing across the classroom "Is it true?" Even worse were the sympathetic head tilts from my teachers, who all made sure I had the grief counselor's name and room number written down. All but Mrs. Blasberg. She just reminded me to study for the trig test next week.

By fourth, I couldn't take it anymore. I texted Sam.

ditching. U in?

Two minutes later she responded with,

totly. 5min bck prklot.

Five minutes later I was standing in the back lot of HHH, scanning the rows of old minivans and compact starter cars for Sam's blond head. Finally, I saw her, bobbing and weaving between the rows, glancing nervously over her shoulder every two seconds.

"We're not dodging the mob, you know," I said when she finally approached. "It's just the faculty."

"Yeah, try explaining that to my dad. I'd get a three-hour lecture on how this is going to play out on my entrance essay to Stanford."

I bit my lip. "Sorry. Wanna go back in?"

She shook her head violently. "H-E-double-hockey-sticks no! I couldn't have been any more avoided today if I'd had swine flu."

"Me, too." I paused. "Josh came over last night."

Sam gave my shoulder a shove. "No way! Tell me!"

I did, quickly filling her in on my midnight visitor, all the while watching her eyes grow wider and wider. By the time I was finished, she looked like she'd been popping No-Doz all morning.

"You seriously promised to help him?" she asked.

I stuck a fingernail between my teeth. Then nodded. "Yeah."

"Dude, Hartley, I thought you were gonna break up with him."

"I know!" I said, a little more loudly than I'd meant to. I made a conscious effort to lower my voice before I continued. "I know. And I did," I assured her, ignoring the memory of how conflicted my stupid emotions had been last night. "But I can tell you there is no way he did this. He may be a cheater and a liar, but he's no killer."

Sam frowned, chewing on this for a moment. "So, what do we do? I mean, it's not like we're investigators or anything."

"No," I hedged, "but think about it—we know HHH inside and out. We have access to all kinds of info about Courtney that no one would ever spill to the cops."

Sam nodded slowly. "True. Okay, so who do we know that hated Courtney?" She paused. "Besides you."

"Gee, thanks."

"You know what I mean."

I pursed my lips. "Well, we could start with the Goths. She was always getting on them for not showing school spirit."

"Oh, and remember how she totally snaked the homecoming crown from that cheerleader with a last-minute voting blitz from the school band?"

I nodded. Truth was, it would be easier to narrow down those who didn't hate Courtney Cline. You didn't get to be that popular by being nice.

"Okay, maybe we need to go at this from a different angle," I decided. "Who had access to the crime scene?"

"Look at you being all *CSI*," Sam teased.

I punched her in the arm. "I'm serious. Who could have been in Josh's house that day?"

"Well, I think we kinda proved it wasn't the Batcave," Sam pointed out. "I mean, anyone could have gotten in the window."

Right. This investigator stuff was harder than it looked.

"Okay, here's what we know," I said. "Courtney was in her Color Guard uniform, right? Which means she took the time to change after school before going to Josh's place. It took us, what, half an hour to get Kevin's car and drive over?"

"At least," Sam agreed.

"And a few minutes to climb the shed."

"Right."

"So, we're looking at a very small window between when school got out at two thirty and when we found her at, say, three fifteen."

"Well, maybe someone in the neighborhood saw something?" Sam offered.

Lightbulb moment.

"The neighbor with the camera!" I pointed my finger at Sam. "The guy in black. He was outside taking pics of his car. Maybe he saw someone go into Josh's house. Maybe he even caught them on camera!"

"Worth a try," Sam said. "Let's go find out."

Since neither of us had any idea what the guy in black's name was, we started by scanning the back parking lot for his dented Camaro. We passed by souped-up pickups belonging to the football team, hand-me-down station wagons driven by the debate team, and a silver sedan with a sparkly purple heart hanging from the rearview that served as the Color Guard's conveyance of choice. But no Camaro. Which meant either (A) his dent damage extended to engine trouble or (B) he was cutting, too. From the bad-boy look he had going on the other day, we took a gamble on (B), and twenty minutes and one bus ride later, we were back on Josh's street. Today, however, his lawn was flattened in patches, showing signs of being trampled by dozens of pairs of feet. A fine sheen of black dust covered the doorjamb and windowsills where finger-prints had no doubt been lifted. And the welcome wreath on the front door was askew, tilting haphazardly to the left.

Josh's Wrangler was conspicuously absent. I sincerely hoped that meant he'd taken off in the middle of the night and not that the cops had confiscated it as evidence.

I marched purposefully down the street, past Josh's, and up the walkway of the house with the Camaro out front, Sam a step behind me. Unlike Josh's, this one had no welcome sign. Instead a "No Soliciting" plaque hung next to the doorbell. In black. With a skull and crossbones on it. I quickly rang the doorbell before I could change my mind.

Two beats later our gamble paid off, and the guy in black opened the door. He looked from Sam to me, recognition immediately dawning. "You two again."

Not the most friendly greeting I'd ever gotten . . .

"Uh, hi. I'm Hartley." I stuck my hand out.

He just looked at it. "Is that the hand that touched the dead girl?"

I pulled it back, rubbing it on the seat of my jeans instead.

Sam took over and waved at him. "I'm Sam."

"Chase," he responded. "I think I've seen you guys around school." Then he paused before adding, "What do you want?"

I shifted from foot to foot on the porch, his directness unnerving me. Not to mention the fact that he looked a lot bigger than I remembered. Taller, more menacing. But he smelled kinda nice, like leather and soap. It was a disturbing combo.

I cleared my throat. "We were wondering if you might have seen anything in the neighborhood while you were taking pictures yesterday."

"What kind of anything?" He crossed his arms over his chest. His very broad chest. He easily could have been on the football team, though I had a feeling from the antiestablishment black and the rebellious guyliner that he wasn't the team spirit type. He seemed more like the playing-depressing-music-in-his-parents'-basement type.

"Anything . . . suspicious? Anyone going in or out of the house down the street?" I clarified.

"You mean other than you two?"

"We didn't kill her!" I said quickly.

He narrowed his eyes. "You sure?"

I threw my hands up. "Yes, I'm sure. Do I look like a killer?"

He let his gaze roll over my body, taking me in from head to toe in a slow assessment that ended in a smirk of approval. I wasn't sure if I should feel flattered or violated.

"That was a rhetorical question," I mumbled, my cheeks heating.

"So, did you?" Sam asked, getting us back on track.

"See anyone go in or out of the house?"

He cocked his head. "Why should I tell you?"

"Uh . . . because . . ." Crap. I hadn't counted on him being so inquisitive. Think fast, girl. "Because . . . we're writing a story for the school's online newspaper. The *Herbert Hoover High Homepage.* And we wanted to get neighbors' reactions to the tragic death." Wow, that didn't sound half bad.

Only I wasn't sure Chase agreed with me. He leaned back on his heels, his mouth curving into a slow smile, his eyes lighting up like he was in on some secret. A really good one.

"What?" I asked.

Instead of answering me, he turned to Sam. "Your friend here is a terrible liar."

I threw my shoulders back. "I am not!"

"You're not what? A liar or a terrible one?"

"Uh . . ." I bit my lip. Okay, in reality I was probably both.

Luckily, Sam jumped in to save me. "What makes you think she's lying?"

"Besides the fact that she's fidgeting on my porch like she's due for a crack fix?"

I froze, forcing my feet to stop shifting.

"I'm not fidgeting," I lied. Again.

"Look, I know you're not from the school newspaper," he went on, "because *I'm* the editor of the *Homepage.*"

Mental forehead smack.

"All right, fine," I finally said. "We're not from the paper."

"Shocker."

I ignored him. "The truth is, Josh is—*was*—my boyfriend."

"So who was the chick you found dead in his bedroom?"

"The girl he was effing," Sam supplied.

Chase did a low whistle before turning to me. "Ouch."

"No kidding. Look, we're just trying to find out what happened."

"Did your boyfriend kill her?" Chase asked.

"No."

"I heard he's missing."

"You did?" I hedged.

"You know where he is?"

"No."

"But you've talked to him?"

"No . . ."

That slow smile spread across his face again. "You really are a terrible liar."

I clenched my jaw, feeling my nostrils flare. "Look, did you see anything yesterday afternoon or not?"

Chase looked from Sam to me, then back again as if trying to decide how much to share. Finally, he seemed to come to a conclusion. "How about I make you guys a deal?"

I almost hated to ask. "A deal?"

"I'll help you with this little investigation you're running and, in exchange, the *Homepage* gets the exclusive story."

I put my hands on my hips. "Like we need your help. We're doing just fine on our own, thank you very much." Another lie. And, from the look on his face, he could tell. I was seriously going to have to work on my poker face.

"You don't like that deal? Fine. How about this one? We all work together, and I don't call the cops and tell them that you're posing as members of the press and interfering with a homicide investigation by harboring the missing boyfriend."

"*Ex*-boyfriend. And I'm not harboring anything." Though I wasn't entirely sure the cops wouldn't see it Chase's way.

"At the very least, you're ditching class," he countered. "Cops don't like that."

"So are you," I quickly pointed out.

"Out sick." He coughed unconvincingly into his hand. Then smirked again. "It's your call, blondie. Me or the cops."

I shifted my weight from foot to foot, weighing the pros and cons. I wasn't hot on the idea of my every move being printed for all HHH society to see. On the other hand, I wasn't so hot on the idea of visiting Josh in a jail cell either.

And, the sad fact was, beyond canvassing the street for any nosy neighbors, I didn't have a clue where to begin a murder investigation. Let's face it, I could use all the help I could get.

I turned to Sam. She cocked her head to the side and shrugged.

"All right. Fine," I said, shoving my hand toward Chase. "Deal."

He grinned, one corner of his mouth tugging upward just a little higher than the other as he grasped my hand and shook.

"Deal."

FIVE

HAVING SEALED MY FATE, FOR BETTER OR WORSE, WE
got right to the point of us being at Chase's in the first
place—the photos Chase was taking outside yesterday
afternoon and whether or not they contained evidence of
the murderer's identity.

"Can we see them?" I asked.

"Why?" he countered.

"We figure Courtney must have been killed between
two thirty and three fifteen," Sam explained. "Which
leaves a small window of opportunity for her killer. If you
were taking pictures then, you might have caught something to help identify him."

He nodded. "I brought my camera out just after school.
Some guy rear-ended me last week. I figured it wouldn't
hurt to have some photographic evidence of the damage.

I was mostly taking close-ups, but you can have a look at them. Come on in."

I hesitated. Something about crossing the threshold felt a little like walking into the lion's den. But, if I wanted to help Josh, I figured Chase was the tamest of the lions I was going to encounter. Besides, we were partners now, right? So I stepped through the doorway a beat after Sam.

The two of us followed Chase into a living room furnished startlingly like my own. A wood entertainment center, housing a pre-HD TV, sat against one wall. A lived-in sofa and love seat combo were situated in front of it for max viewing pleasure. To the right a kitchen tiled in baby blue was just visible beyond an oak dinette set. All standard suburban issue.

We followed Chase up the stairs and to the left, down a short hallway with three rooms branching off. Chase ushered us into the second one on the right, pushing open a white wooden door with a "Keep Out" sign on it.

Here the decor was much more teen angst than happy homemaker, making it clear that Chase's mom did, in fact, adhere to the sign on the door. The walls were painted in black, creating a cavelike effect. A fuzzy black blanket covered the bed, and a closet full of black clothes spanned the back wall, shirts and jeans dangling askew on overburdened hangers. On the walls were posters of bands I'd never heard of, their singers' tongues protruding, war paint on their faces, fake blood dripping from their mouths. Charming.

One window faced south, a pair of dark curtains pulled shut. Black ones. (Gee, what a surprise.) It was nearing noon outside, but in here it was midnight. I squinted in the darkness, feeling my pupils enlarge to find some little pinpoint of light to glom onto.

A gunmetal gray desk sat in the corner. Strewn across its top were a laptop, a digital camera, and a collection of different lenses. Chase went straight to the desk, flipping open his laptop.

"Have a seat. This will just take a minute," Chase offered.

I looked around. A desk chair littered with black clothes sat to one side. Beside it a wooden folding chair piled high with school textbooks. Which just left the bed. I scooted a couple pillows aside and gingerly perched on the edge.

Or *tried* to gingerly perch on the edge.

The second my butt hit the fuzzy black blanket, I sank down half a dozen inches, the mattress wobbling like I'd planted myself on Jell-O.

"Whoa!" Sam said, mirroring my own surprise as she sat beside me. "Water bed."

"Nice, huh?" Chase asked over his shoulder.

"Fab." I felt my cheeks go warm, trying not to think about the kind of action that went on in a bed like this, and scooted closer to the edge.

I struggled to maintain a vertical position, swaying next to Sam, as I watched Chase click away on his computer. Soon, an array of thumbnails filled the screen, showing his dented bumper from fifteen different angles. Most were indeed close-ups, displaying bashed-in chrome and a crushed taillight, but a few caught a glimpse of the street beyond in the background.

"Can you make those bigger?" I asked, pointing to a couple where I could almost make out the corner of Josh's house.

"I can do anything you want with them," he answered, immediately enlarging the images.

Sam and I leaned forward, squinting at the screen. Around large-scale bits of bumper I could make out a few trees, the garage of the house next door, the front of Josh's Jeep. In a couple of photos the other cars parked across the street were visible. In another, the tires of Sam's brother's SVO Volvo peeked into the frame.

But unfortunately nothing screamed "murderer" or "smoking gun."

I wasn't entirely sure what I'd hoped to see on the photos, but clearly Chase's camera hadn't picked up anything incriminating.

"I hate to say it, but I don't really see anything here," Sam said, voicing my own disappointment.

"Sorry," Chase responded, shutting the window. "I told you they were mostly close-ups."

"So now what?" I asked.

Chase pulled a wide-ruled notebook and a pen from a backpack beside his desk. "I think we should make a list of everyone who had issues with Courtney." He paused. Then gave me a pointed look. "Besides you."

I rolled my eyes.

"Yeah, we thought of that already," Sam told him. "The problem is, we couldn't figure out who *didn't* have issues with Courtney." She paused. "You got any guesses?"

He shook his head. "We didn't really run in the same social circles. I knew who she was, but she was a year behind me, so I never had much to do with her."

Which made Chase a senior and explained why Sam and I had never had much to do with him either. The divide between class years was almost as wide as the gap between the all-black-all-the-time crowd and the perktastic Color Guard girls.

I watched as Chase pursed his lips, his eyebrows hunkering together. I noticed his eyebrows were a lot darker than Josh's. Almost bordering on too full, but instead of looking unkempt they gave off a thoughtful vibe. Like he spent a lot of time contemplating the secrets of the universe.

Or maybe just the secrets of death metal lyrics.

"Let's go talk to her friends," he finally said. "They'd

know if Courtney had been having issues with anyone in particular lately."

I slipped my cell from my pocket, checking the time. 11:45. Almost lunch. It was as good a time as any to catch the Color Guard girls for a chat.

Chase grabbed a hoodie from his closet—black with a big purple eagle on the back—and led the way back through the house to the front door.

There was just one problem.

Sam and I were sans transportation. And the bus didn't come by again for another half hour, by which time the Color Guard girls would be safely tucked away in fifth period. If we wanted to question them before the end of the day, we had only one alternative.

I stared at Chase's dented Camaro in the driveway.

"It's just a scratch. She still runs fine," he assured us, pulling open the passenger-side door.

The dented bumper leaned to one side, the muffler tilting precariously close to the ground. If I sneezed, I was pretty sure the tailpipe would fall off.

"So, some guy hit you from behind?" I asked.

"Yeah. Total jerk. But it was the guy in front of me that really caused the accident. He stopped suddenly, I braked, and the guy behind me rammed my tail."

"Oh." I felt a little better. Sudden stop slamage could happen to anyone, right? I pushed the front seat forward, climbing over it into the tiny back. "So it wasn't your fault."

Chase shook his head. "Nope. Totally the guy in front of me. I mean, who stops for a yellow light, ya know?"

Oh no.

I opened my mouth to protest that maybe the bus wouldn't be so bad after all, but I didn't get a chance as Chase slammed the door shut. Sam slid into the front, and I tried to swallow my concern as Chase started the car. But it kinda stuck in my throat as he peeled out of the driveway and took the first corner on two tires.

"Um, so, how long have you had your license?" I asked, gripping the armrest on the door like a life preserver.

"Since last year. Spent my sixteenth birthday in line at the DMV."

"Really?" I felt the seat belt go taut against my chest as he took another corner at NASCAR speeds. "Did you, uh, pass on the first try?"

"Of course."

He went over a speed bump, and I swear we caught at least two feet of air. I felt my head kiss the ceiling.

"And how many accidents have you been in?"

"Just one."

That was a small comfort.

"This month," he added.

I closed my eyes and said a silent prayer to the gods of clear intersections.

Luckily, we arrived back at Herbert Hoover High in one piece (though I was pretty sure Mr. Chase's wild ride had shaved a good five years off my life). We turned onto High School Drive (geniusly named, no?) just as classes were letting out for a fifty-five minute lunch period and pulled into the school's back parking lot. Which, at this time of day, was a drive-at-your-own-risk zone. Brand-new drivers in SUVs and hand-me-down sedans filled the lot, furiously texting despite hands-free laws as they rushed to Starbucks for a quick caffeine fix. Each car was filled to capacity, and the sounds of dueling mp3s blasting from souped-up stereos filled the air—Taylor Swift warring with Usher over the indistinguishable deep bass of a hip-hop song.

Chase seemed oblivious to the dangers of three hundred newbie drivers all cramming into one lot at the same time, his Camaro flying over the speed bumps like a bad seventies cop show. My teeth chattered together as I again caught air in my seat.

"You know, you're supposed to slow down for speed bumps," I offered.

"Where's the fun in that?" Chase grinned at me in the rearview mirror.

I gritted my teeth, praying I would make it with all my fillings intact.

After narrowly avoiding a collision with a Honda Accord carrying half the debate team, Chase pulled his car into a slot near the field.

As Chase locked up his death trap and we crossed the parking lot, I caught a glimpse of Detective Raley hovering near the cafeteria. He had a member of the school band cornered, questioning him with an intensity that had the poor guy pinned. I hated to break it to the detective, but if Courtney had said more than boo to a band member all year, I'd eat my chem book. He was seriously barking up the wrong tree.

I had much higher hopes for our prey as Chase led the way into the HHH main quad where the Color Guard girls held midday court.

When I'd first started at HHH, Mom had suggested I try out for "that cheerleading with flags." It had taken me the better part of a gluten-free soy burger to explain to her the intricate and seriously important differences between cheerleaders and Color Guard girls.

Cheer was for girls who liked to shake their butts and do splits in short skirts in front of a screaming crowd. Color Guard was for good girls who had more school spirit than brains. Cheerleaders dated college guys with tattoos. Color Guard girls dated guys with trust funds. The last four girls in our school's own "sixteen and pregnant" club were cheerleaders. The last four presidents of the Chastity Club had been Color Guard girls. Cheerleaders were the future Playmates of the world. Color Guard girls grew up to be soccer moms with Louis Vuitton diaper bags.

Needless to say, neither had been a group I'd been dying to join as a freshman, and I had never regretted that decision.

The cheerleaders usually spent their lunch break off campus, smoking Marlboro lights (to stay thin). The Color Guard girls, on the other hand, took the prime spot under the lone shade tree in the quad at the center of school, drinking Sugarfree Red Bull (to stay thin). (Okay, maybe they did have one or two things in common.)

Usually the conversation from the Color Guard camp could be heard from two buildings over, since the cooler the person perceived herself to be the louder she chatted. But as we approached today, the group was unusually subdued in deference to the passing of their queen. Girls gathered in twos and threes to voice their theories about her death in stage whispers. I noticed black bands covering the upper arms of several of them, though instead of the usual plain cotton, these were shot through with sparkly purple threads. Designer mourning bands. How appropriate.

In the center of the mix, surrounded by at least a dozen future soccer moms, sat Courtney's two best friends—Caitlyn Calvin and Kaylee Clark. If you've ever seen a Barbie doll, you've seen Caitlyn and Kaylee. Straight, shiny blond hair loaded with enough product to create their very own ozone holes. Big blue eyes rimmed in eyeliner, mascara, eye shadow, and then a little more mascara for good measure. Complexions as perfect as a Proactiv after photo and their limbs an even honey color that somehow looked natural despite the absence of any tan lines.

Clearly every girl on campus simultaneously hated them and wanted to be them.

Caitlyn was dressed in a white skirt that came to mid-thigh (just low enough to pass dress code but high enough to show off the fruits of her Red Bull addiction), a tank top with ruffles down the front in a pale violet version of the Color Guard's mandatory purple, and a pair of white canvas Skechers that somehow defied any sign of dirt. Beside her, Kaylee wore a carbon copy of the outfit, only her tank was more of an indigo purple. The only thing to differentiate Thing One from Thing Two was that Caitlyn's hair was pulled back from her face on the right side with a purple clip. Kaylee's was pulled back on the left.

Caitlyn, right—Kaylee, left, I chanted to myself as we approached them.

I felt conversation around us fall from a stage whisper to a heavy silence as I walked up, a clear sign I'd been the topic. I ducked my head, not wanting to make eye contact.

Chase, on the other hand, walked right up to the gruesome twosome, oblivious to the stares, and abruptly halted conversations as an intruder invaded their ranks.

"Caitlyn?" Chase asked.

Thing One gave him a slow up and down, her blue eyes silently assessing whether or not he was worthy of an answer. While his black-on-black style probably wasn't up to her standards, a tiny smile curved the corner of her mouth as she took in the broad shoulders, dark eyes, square jaw. He might not be a trust-fund baby, but he had enough of the brooding bad boy thing going on to arouse her interest. Or at least, I assumed he did as Caitlyn answered, "That's me. And you are . . . ?"

"Chase Erikson."

Caitlyn shot him a big smile that spoke to the fact she was a lot more vigilant about wearing her retainer at night than I was. "Nice to meet you, Chase," she said, her voice purring over his name as she twirled a lock of blond hair between her fingers. "What can I do for you?"

"I'm with the *Herbert Hoover High Homepage*."

She gave him a blank look.

"The school's online paper."

She shrugged. "'Kay." Clearly she was not the reading kind.

"I was wondering if I could ask you a few questions about Courtney?"

Caitlyn lowered her eyes to the ground, doing an exaggerated sniff. "I don't know. It's all so raw. I can't believe she's really gone." Sniff, sniff.

"I can answer for you," Kaylee piped up, her eyes locked onto Chase's biceps like they were éclairs and her underweight self had spent the school year existing on . . . well . . . Sugarfree Red Bull.

Caitlyn shot Thing Two a dirty look. "I didn't say I couldn't answer. It's just hard." She turned back to Chase. "She was my best friend, you know."

Chase nodded.

"She was my best friend, too!" Kaylee piped up, determined not to be left out. Then she did an exact replica of Caitlyn's sniff thing.

"When was the last time you saw your best friend?" he asked the pair.

Caitlyn drew her perfectly threaded eyebrows together. "Yesterday. After school."

"What time?" I chimed in. If we knew exactly when Courtney left, it would help narrow down the time of her death.

Caitlyn's eyes cut to me, blinking as if seeing me for the first time. "I dunno. After school. We saw her right before Color Guard practice."

"Did she seem upset by anything?" Chase asked. "Or distracted? Preoccupied?"

Caitlyn shook her head. "No, she was perfectly fine. Her usual self."

"Was she having problems with anyone?" he pressed. "Anyone have a reason to be upset with her that you know of? Anyone with a reason to want her dead?"

Caitlyn's eyes shot my way.

"Besides me," I quickly added.

She shrugged. "I don't know."

"I do," Kaylee cut in.

Caitlyn sent her a look, but Kaylee marched on, undeterred. Clearly a cute bad boy trumped the Color Guard
code of loyalty. "I know who killed her."

I raised an eyebrow. Surely it wasn't going to be that
easy, was it?

"Who?" Chase asked.

"Josh DuPont," she announced. Then executed another
perfect sniff. "He killed my best friend."

"No way!" I shouted automatically.

Chase shot me a silent warning look, before turning
back to Kaylee. "Why do you say that?" he pressed.

"She got a text from him just before school let out,"
Kaylee explained.

I felt my stomach clench. "Are you sure?"

She nodded. "Positive. She read it to me."

"What did it say?" Chase asked.

"He wanted her to meet him at his house after school."

I bit my lip. "It didn't happen to say why, did it? Like,
maybe she was helping him with a science project about
condoms?"

Chase and Sam turned to me as one. Both wearing the
same "get real" looks on their faces that said they pitied

my stint in la-la land.

"What? It's possible . . ." I mumbled to a spot of lint on my sleeve.

Chase turned his attention back to the Abercrombie twins. "So, the rumors were true? Courtney was sleeping with Josh?"

I cringed at the directness of his question. Mostly because it begged a direct answer. One I wasn't sure I wanted to face head-on while standing in front of the entire Color Guard squad.

I could feel the eyes of every purple-clad girl giving me a critical assessment, silently comparing me to their late queen and wondering just how long it would have taken Josh to choose between us. I wore jeans. Courtney had worn designer denim with her initials monogrammed on the pockets in purple sparkly thread. I wore sneakers. She'd worn Ed Hardy athletic shoes with rhinestones embedded along the tongue. I had inherited what Mom liked to call an "athletic" build. She had looked like she was smuggling water balloons in her top. While my self-esteem was generally pretty healthy, I felt it wavering uncomfortably as speculation burned into me from fifteen different sets of judgmental eyes.

Luckily, it was speculation that would go unanswered.

Kaylee opened her mouth to speak again, but before she could answer Chase's question, Caitlyn rode right over her.

"There is absolutely no way Courtney was sleeping with Josh. She wasn't sleeping with anyone. Courtney was a virgin."

Sam let out a loud snort.

Caitlyn turned on her the way a lion might turn on a juicy steak. "Don't you dare disparage her good name!" she warned.

I was impressed. *Disparage* was a top ten SAT vocab word. Someone had been working with her tutor.

"I wouldn't dream of it," Sam promised, holding her hands up in a surrender motion. Then muffled another snicker.

"Courtney signed the chastity pledge on the first day of freshman year," Caitlyn continued. "No way would she go back on it. She took it very seriously. Courtney was a virgin. I'd stake my life on it." She turned to Chase. "And you can print that."

But he didn't look so convinced. "If that's true, why was she meeting Josh in his bedroom yesterday afternoon?"

Caitlyn shrugged her bony shoulders. "I don't know. Why don't you ask him?"

Trust me, I intended to.

SIX

THE BELL FOR FIFTH PERIOD RANG, AND STUDENTS immediately ran inside, Sam included, calling over her shoulder that she had a Spanish test that afternoon. Me? I'd already ruined my perfect attendance record by cutting that morning. I didn't really see any sense in finishing out the day. Especially when (A) I'd blown off my homework last night so I didn't have anything to turn in, and (B) there was zero chance of me being able to concentrate anyway. Not when Detective Raley was lurking in the halls, Josh was on the run, and the entire HHH student body couldn't decide whether I'd killed Courtney or had been about to be dumped for her. Or both.

What I needed to do was to speak to Josh. If he really had texted Courtney, effectively luring her to her death, I needed to know why. Yes, I was aware that the obvious answer was, duh, booty call. But I held out hope that all was not as obvious as it seemed. What can I say? I'm a big fan of denial.

Considering Raley was likely watching my cell usage like a hawk, I didn't dare contact Josh via my phone. Instead, I decided to walk the two blocks to the public library on Main and mooch off their free internet to get in touch with him.

I turned to go . . .

And almost ran smack into Chase's chest.

Apparently not *everyone* had dispersed at the sound of the bell.

"Going to class?" he asked.

No. But he didn't need to know that. Considering I wasn't exactly sure what sort of answers I might get from Josh, I didn't really want an audience. Besides, I wasn't certain I totally trusted Chase. When push came to shove, Chase had no loyalty to me. He was in this for a story. And he got that story whether Josh went to jail or not.

So instead of spilling my destination, I nodded. Slowly. "Yes. Yes, I am going to class."

He grinned. "Dude, you are the worst liar on the planet. Seriously, we got to get you some lessons or something."

I rolled my eyes. "Whatever." I pushed past him, heading toward the front of the school.

"So, if you're not going to class, what are you doing?"

he persisted, following a step behind me.

"Nothing."

"Where are you going?"

"Nowhere."

"Need a ride to nowhere?"

"No!" Even if I did, I wasn't ready to take my life in my hands by riding with him twice in one day. "Look, just because we're both investigating this thing doesn't mean we have to be joined at the hip."

Chase stopped following me. He gave me a long look. Then grinned again.

"Okay. Fine. I'll catch you later, then."

"Fine. Good. Catch ya." I turned to go again.

And heard him call over my shoulder, "Say hi to Josh for me!"

Sigh.

The local branch of our library was situated just down the street from the high school. In theory it was within convenient walking distance for students looking to study after class. In reality, it smelled like musty paper, mildewed carpets, and unwashed bodies. Needless to say, everyone under the age of sixty avoided it like the plague. It was a squat concrete block of a building, boasting the latest in "modern architecture," circa nineteen fifty. Orange carpet covered the walls (yes, the *walls*) and beige linoleum the floors. Metal racks held books still organized via card catalog, despite the availability of digital sorting. The town kept threatening to update the library, posting fancy watercolor renderings of the new building in the paper every year. But as of yet, fund-raising had only reached the level of enthusiasm necessary to pay for the watercolors, not the real building.

I held my breath as I pushed through the glass front doors, slipping past the circulation desk and heading downstairs to the basement that housed periodicals and two rows of ancient PCs. Laminated signs next to each station warned that we were only allowed one hour of internet usage at a time. With any luck, I'd only need a fraction of that.

I settled down at a station next to a white-haired woman looking at pictures of her grandkids on Photobucket (letting out the occasional coo at how cute they were) and a guy wearing three coats, two pairs of socks, and a week-old beard. I made sure to sit upwind from the overdressed guy, then logged online and made my way to MySpace to find the fake account that Josh had set up last night.

Honestly, I hadn't been on MySpace in years, not since fourth grade. As soon as Jessica Hanson had enticed me to join her mafia, I'd been strictly a Facebook user. But, as Josh had pointed out, if everyone was on Facebook, MySpace was the virtual equivalent of a hideout in the woods. Deep, deserted woods.

I clicked on HHHRunner94 and came to a page tricked

out with a red background, flaming cursors, and about twenty different songs on an automatic playlist. Granny shot me a look as the Kings of Leon blasted from the PC speakers. I quickly hit Mute, sending her an apologetic smile. Clearly being on the run left Josh with way too much time on his hands.

I scrolled down, hitting the Message Me button shaped like a skull and crossbones (Really, Josh? That didn't strike you as just a little bit inappropriate?) and typed a quick note into the message window. I kept it short and cryptic on the off chance that Raley had somehow cracked Josh's online alias.

Need to talk. Be online 2nite. 9 p.m.

I hit Send, hoping Josh was monitoring the account as vigilantly as he'd promised, then packed up my stuff and headed home.

To kill a few more minutes, I stopped at Jamba Juice for a Peach Pleasure smoothie. School wasn't technically out yet, and the last thing I wanted was the third degree from Mom on why I was early. Which, as it turned out, was the least of my worries. When I turned the corner onto my street, I spied an unmarked beige sedan with police lights on the dash parked squarely in front of my house.

Raley.

I closed my eyes and thought a really bad word as I did

a mental assessment of the situation. If Raley was inside, he was likely talking to Mom. The upside? If they were talking about murder, she probably wasn't going to focus on the fact that I was home a little early. The downside? Mom tended to be a tad overprotective. And by a "tad," I mean I was seven before she let me go down the twisty slide at the park for fear of "owies." I could only imagine how she'd take this.

I had a fleeting fantasy of just turning around and walking away. Hiding out at the mall for, oh, say, the rest of my life. But it was short-lived. Anyway, it was a total pipe dream to think that Mom wouldn't find out about Courtney's death. I mean, hello? A girl at our school was murdered. Of course she would find out. In fact, I was sorta surprised it had taken this long. While Mom never watched the news (she said all that negativity interrupted the flow of her chi), she was as connected to the momvine as someone could be.

And clearly Raley was giving her the gossip motherlode.

I took a deep, fortifying breath and forged up the flagstone pathway to my front door. I opened it to find Mom and Detective Raley in the living room—Detective Raley standing near the empty fireplace, Mom perched on the edge of our brown microfiber sofa, her forehead etched with a line of concern I'd grown to know well. It was the same one she'd flashed at me when I pointed to the twisty slide, the same one she'd pulled out when I'd taken up Tae Kwon Do in third grade, and the same one that had frozen on her features all through driver's ed last spring. It was her SMother face.

And it was never good.

As soon as she spotted me, she popped up from the sofa and crossed the four steps to the door to tackle me like a linebacker.

"Oh, Hartley, honey, are you okay?" she mumbled into my hair.

"Mom, I think you're breaking my ribs."

She eased up on her grip, stepping back to look at me as if finding a dead girl might leave a mark. "Detective Raley told me everything. Oh, honey, why didn't you say anything? How awful for you!"

I shot Raley a look, wondering just how much "everything" was, but his face was a blank, unreadable thing.

"I'm fine," I lied.

"Fine? My God, your friend was killed, Hart. Clearly you're not fine."

I didn't point out that Courtney and I were hardly BFFs. In Mom's world everyone under the age of eighteen was friends with everyone else, like we were all part of some secret society of minors.

"Really, I'm okay."

"Good. Then you won't mind answering a few

questions," Raley said.

For a brief moment I thought about faking hysteria to avoid his interrogation. Maybe I *wasn't* fine. Maybe we *were* BFFs. Maybe I *did* need a few more SMotherly hugs.

But since I knew Raley wasn't really giving me a say in the matter, I nodded mutely and sat down on the sofa to face the music. Mom sat next to me and patted my hand.

"When was the last time you saw Josh?" Raley started.

"Yesterday," I said slowly. Which was the truth.

"What time?"

"Early." Which was definitely *not* the truth. I prayed I wasn't as bad at lying as Chase seemed to think I was.

"Can you be more specific?" Raley pressed.

"Before school."

"*Before* school?" Raley asked, raising one eyebrow.

"Yup." I nodded so hard my hair fell in my eyes. Which was just as well, because if I lifted them to meet his, I'm pretty sure he would be able to tell I was on the downside of truthful.

"Okay." Raley scribbled something in his notebook.

I leaned forward to see if it was "liar, liar, pants on fire," but he turned the page before I could make it out.

"Any idea where Josh might be now?" he asked.

I shook my head. This time I was being 100 percent truthful. Of course, he hadn't asked if I knew how to contact Josh later tonight . . .

"Wait—" my mom said, holding up one hand. "What do you mean, 'might be'? Is he missing?"

"He's not at home, ma'am," Raley answered non-committally.

"As in missing?" Her voice rose an octave.

"We don't have information about his current where-abouts," Raley said carefully, though he looked straight at me when he said it. I averted my gaze, finding an incred-ibly interesting stain on the carpet.

"Is he in danger?" she asked.

"We don't believe that's likely," he hedged.

"So . . . if you don't believe he's in danger . . ." Mom said, trailing off as I watched her mental hamster jump on his little wheel. Mom may be a little quirky, but she's no dummy.

"Josh is a 'person of interest' in this case," Raley said, doing his air quotes thing again.

Mom leaned forward in her seat, a hand going to her chest. "You're not saying Josh had anything to do with this, are you?"

"We're exploring all possibilities," Raley said. "At this time, we'd really like to talk to the boy. If you have any idea where he might be . . ." His eyes bored holes into me.

My eyes? Still glued to the carpet stain. You know, it kind of resembled a fish on its side. Mom might want to think about getting it steam cleaned sometime soon.

"We have no idea. We haven't seen him since . . ." Mom turned to me.

"Yesterday. Before school," I repeated. Unfortunately no more convincingly than the last time.

"Oh, Hartley," Mom said, hugging me again. "To think I let you go out with a killer!"

"Mom!" I squirmed out of her grasp. "He didn't kill Courtney."

"It could have been you, Hart."

"It could *not* have been me. Because he didn't do it."

"Should I call his parents?" Mom asked, looking at the cordless on the end table.

"His parents have been notified about the situation," Raley told her. "They're currently on a cruise in Alaska, but will be flying in as soon as the ship docks at the next port."

"God, I can't believe it. I played tennis with Josh's mom just last month," Mom said. "And here she was, raising a murderer."

"Mom!"

"Hartley, we have several witnesses that say you were upset after school yesterday," Raley said, jumping in.

I narrowed my eyes. "Upset?"

"Angry."

"Who said?"

"Witnesses."

"You know teenagers—they tend to be a little overdramatic."

He narrowed his eyes at me. "Considering the drama—overdone as it may have been—let's say Josh knew how upset you were. Knew that you intended to confront Courtney, thought Courtney would come clean to you about their relationship. Let's say he didn't want that. Let's say he decided Courtney needed to be kept quiet."

I pursed my lips. Since he hadn't phrased it as a question, I didn't feel compelled to answer.

"Relationship? What relationship?" Mom asked.

As far as Mom knew, *my* entire relationship with Josh consisted of movies at the mall and holding hands at the school dances. I was pretty sure that she was as acquainted with denial as I was when it came to teen sex.

Which is why when Raley opened his mouth to answer, I jumped in first.

"Science partner! Courtney was working on a science project with him. About reproduction."

Raley raised an eyebrow at me. But thankfully he let it go.

"Is it safe to send Hartley to school?" Mom asked. "Maybe I should keep her home for a few days."

"I'm sure it's safe for her to return to school."

"But wasn't she some sort of witness?"

"After the fact."

"Do witnesses after the fact need witness protection?"

I rolled my eyes.

I could see Raley resisting the urge to do the same.

"I believe she's safe, Mrs. Featherstone. This feels like an isolated incident."

"I saw a TV show about this on Lifetime just the other day. The woman went into witness protection, but the killer found her anyway. What if the killer finds her anyway? What guarantee do you have that she'll be safe?"

"I assure you that we're doing all we can to find the person who committed this crime, Mrs. Featherstone."

"You mean Josh."

But Raley had mastered the art of noncommittal. "I'm sure once we talk to Mr. DuPont, he'll be able to clear up quite a few things for us."

You and me both, pal.

SEVEN

ONCE RALEY LEFT, MOM JUMPED RIGHT INTO THE kitchen, making me comfort food that she insisted I needed after my "harrowing brush with death." I thought about telling her that rice noodle macaroni with soy cheese was not exactly my idea of comfort, but I figured it was easier to let her cook her anxiety away.

Not that that stopped her from going into overprotective mode with a vengeance when my dad called.

"She may need witness protection!" she yelled into the phone.

"I'm fine, Mom!" I said.

"She said she's fine," Mom relayed into the receiver, "but I don't think she is. She looks pale."

"I'm right here, you know."

"I'm worried about her, Brian. I think maybe we

should go away for a while. Maybe we should go stay at my mother's."

I did an internal shudder. I'd already spent four weeks this summer surrounded by Bengay and Polident. That was more than anyone deserved in one calendar year. "Mom, I'm fine, I swear," I said, around a bite of mac and faux cheese. I shoveled more noodles into my mouth as if to prove my point. "See? Fine."

A plate and a half later I finally managed to convince Mom I was duly comforted, not about to be hacked to death by my boyfr—er, *ex*-boyfriend—and fine to attend school tomorrow.

I rinsed my dishes off and hightailed it to my room to escape further coddling.

8:06.

I logged onto MySpace, just in case Josh was early, then hunkered down to wait.

I surfed TMZ and the *L.A. Informer* websites for the latest celebrity news. Harvested some pineapples on Farm Town. Checked what movies were playing downtown this weekend. Watched mudkiplover08's latest video on YouTube. Took a blog poll about what brand of lip gloss tastes the best.

8:32.

Out of other time wasters, I logged onto the HHH website to check what today's homework was. Study notes for a history quiz on Monday, sentences to diagram for English, and three pages of equations from Mrs. Blasberg. Fab. I pulled my books out of my backpack and figured I might as well attempt to pass my classes this semester. Unfortunately, I had a hard time concentrating when my entire being was focused on watching for that little "online now" icon to appear next to Josh's name. I worked with one eye on the clock, one eye on my screen, sending random glances toward my paper as I solved sentences and diagrammed equations. Or maybe it was the other way around. Like I said, I wasn't really paying that close attention.

8:59

I finished my trig and English and took up vigil at my computer.

9:02

Come on, Josh, where are you?

9:08

I started chanting, "Log on, log on, log on, log on" to the tune of "I'm a Little Teapot."

9:12

Maybe he didn't get my message earlier. Maybe he wasn't watching the MySpace account after all. Maybe he created it and forgot about it. Maybe Raley had nabbed him and he was sitting in a jail cell right now, rotting away, wishing his girlfr—*ex*-girlfriend—had been more vigilant about finding Courtney's real killer.

Hey.

I let out a sigh of relief so loud I feared Mom would hear it over her Exercise TV On Demand downstairs.

You're late.

Sorry. Had 2 find a computer.

Where did u find one?

Apple store. I'm "testing" one out. Don't have much time b4 salesguy catches on.

I couldn't help a little grin. Very inventive.

What's up? he asked.

That was a loaded question. But, considering he had an employee working on commission hovering over his shoulder, I decided to get right to the point.

Did you text Courtney yesterday?

There was a pause on his end. I hoped it meant he was trying to remember and not that his test-drive time had expired.

Why? he finally typed

Hmm . . . answering a question with a question. Classic evasion tactic. Not that I was falling for it.

Caitlyn said you texted CC after school. True?

This time his answer was immediate.

No.

I felt a sigh of relief escape me.

Really? You didn't send her a text? Telling her to meet at your house?

NO!

Okay, it didn't mean the whole condom-in-the-locker and rumor-mill things were total crap, but at least my faith in his innocence wasn't totally misplaced.

Then who sent the text?

I dunno. Someone is trying to set me up.

And doing a good job of it if the detective stalking me was any indication.

Why?

I don't know. But I swear I didnt tell Corntey to meet at my house.

I ignored the spelling mistake, instead pursing my lips and digesting this information. Did I believe him? Mostly. Probably. Maybe. He hadn't racked up a whole lot of points in the trustworthy department lately.

On the other hand, it was pretty convenient how all evidence led straight to Josh. Too convenient. And, as anyone who has ever watched TV knows, when a trail of clues seems too good to be true, it usually is.

Still there? Josh typed.

I nodded at the screen.

Ya.

Miss u.

I bit my lip. And told myself to ignore the way my stomach suddenly felt warm and squishy. I didn't care if he missed me. I didn't care what he felt. He had no feelings as far as I was concerned. Neither did I. This was about finding a killer. Not about missing anyone.

I have to go, I typed.

W8!

What?

Thnx. ur the best.

I quickly logged off before I could type anything stupid back.

Like, I miss you, too.

EIGHT

"MY PARENTS THREATENED TO SEND ME TO A CONVENT."
Sam took a bite of her egg salad sandwich, a small glob of
mayo hanging on the corner of her mouth. "And we're not
even Catholic!"

I shook my head in sympathy. "Dude."

After his chat with my mother, Raley had visited Sam's
parents, giving them much the same sort of heart attack
he'd given my mom. Only Sam's parents were already in
hyperprotective mode, having seen Courtney's picture on
the ten o'clock news. If my mom was afraid of negative
energy, Sam's parents ate it up like it was fuel. They even
had a map posted on their kitchen wall with little pushpins
stuck in it where, according to the Megan's law website,
every registered sex offender within ten miles of their
house lived. Needless to say, those streets were blocked

out in red as routes Sam was not allowed to take to school.

"Did Raley give you the third degree?" I asked, breaking into my Red Delicious apple.

Sam nodded, her tongue whipping out to remove the mayo glob. "And fourth and fifth. God, you'd think I was the one who killed her, the way he grilled me. I was an innocent witness!" she said. Then she paused. "Well, almost innocent. He told my dad that we snuck in Josh's window."

I cringed. "Ouch. What did your dad say?"

"That Stanford does not let breakers and enterers into their premed program." She paused. "I'm paraphrasing here. It was hard to make out the exact words, what with all the shouting."

"Sucks," I said.

"No kidding. Did you talk to Josh last night?" Sam asked, reaching into her brown bag for a napkin.

I glanced up. The cafeteria was crowded, but most people were paying more attention to their taco platters than the conversation around them. Still, I leaned in, whispering my answer, lest Raley somehow pry the info out of the masses.

"Yeah."

"Did you see him?"

I shook my head. "We IM'd."

"Good. Then you aren't technically aiding and abetting."

I raised an eyebrow at her.

"That's what Raley told my dad last night. That if I knew if you knew where Josh was I had better tell him because it meant I was concealing information about someone aiding and abetting. He seemed pretty serious."

I blew out a breath, ruffling my hair. "I know. Which is why I had to talk to Josh about the text Courtney got."

She shoved a straw into a juice box, sipping grape juice into her mouth. "So, what did he say? Did he send it?"

I shook my head, and quickly relayed the conversation with Josh.

"If he didn't send it, who did?"

I shrugged. "Obviously someone who wanted to make it look like it was from Josh. Someone who heard the rumor that Josh and Courtney were . . . you know."

"Effing?"

I cringed. "Yeah."

Sam looked around the room. "I hate to tell you this, Hart, but that doesn't narrow the field down a whole lot. Pretty much everyone had heard by then."

I pulled my pride up off the bottom of my shoe. "Thanks. I needed that reminder."

Sam ignored me, instead tilting her head toward the front of the cafeteria. "Don't look now, but here comes our 'partner.'"

Of course I couldn't help swiveling in my seat to get a

better view of the front entrance.

Where Chase was framed in the doorway.

His broad shoulders filled the entryway almost as tightly as anyone on the HHH football team's would. He was tall, but not in a gangly way, and he had muscles pumped up in all the right places. He was wearing a pair of jeans and was once again doing the black T-shirt thing. He had on a pair of black Docs, a black leather cuff on his right wrist, and his black hair was spiked up from his head in a mussed kind of way. Not crusty straight, but more bedroom tousled.

Not that I had any firsthand knowledge of what bedroom tousled might look like, but I imagined that was it.

Um, wow. Chase was actually kinda hot.

I mean, if you went for that whole bad boy thing. Which I totally didn't. Bad boys were bad, and I'd had enough bad boyfriend to last me a lifetime, thank you very much.

Chase's eyes scanned the room and found mine staring back at him.

I blushed. God knows why.

Luckily he didn't seem to notice and made a beeline toward our table.

"Oh, great. Here he comes," Sam said, completely oblivious to the heat in my cheeks.

She put her head down, sucking loudly through her straw.

"Hey," Chase said, planting himself on the bench next to me.

"Hey," I said back.

"Any luck contacting your boyfriend?" he asked.

"*Ex*-boyfriend," I emphasized.

"Whatever." He waved the technicality off. "So? You talk to him?"

I shrugged. "Sorta."

Considering Raley was systematically threatening all my friends with criminal charges, admitting outright that I was in contact with a fugitive didn't seem like all that clever of a plan.

"Sorta? What's that mean?" Chase asked. He looked down at the uneaten taco on my plate and, without even asking, picked it up and took a huge bite.

Okay, I totally wasn't planning on eating the beef(ish) taco. (And if you're not sure why, notice the *ish* part.) But it was pretty presumptuous of him. And kinda intimate. For some reason it made my cheeks heat even more.

"It means Josh didn't send the text," I answered, watching him chew.

"You sure?" Chase cocked an eyebrow at me.

"Positive."

"He told you that?"

I bit my lip. "Just trust me. He didn't send it."

"O-kay." Though the still-cocked eyebrow clearly didn't believe me.

"So," I forged ahead, "either Caitlyn is lying to us about the text, or Courtney lied to her."

"Or Josh is lying to you," Chase pointed out. He paused. "Or you're lying to us."

I narrowed my eyes at him. "And why would I do that?"

"I don't know. Why would you try to prove the innocence of a guy who cheated on you?"

I bit my lip. I was not dignifying that question with an answer. Especially not while he was eating *my* taco.

"My relationship with Josh is private," I told him.

He grinned. "Dude, there's nothing private about that relationship now. Everyone in school knows your business."

"My name is not 'Dude,'" I said. "And all you need to know about Josh is that he's innocent."

Chase gave me a long look. "Girls really will believe anything, won't they?"

I narrowed my eyes at him again. Then moved my plate out of his reach.

"Look, there's one way to find out for sure who's telling the truth," Sam said, clearly trying to play peacemaker before someone took a taco to the head. "Courtney's phone would have a record of who sent all the texts."

"Yeah, except that her phone is probably in the hands

of the police right now," I pointed out.

"Right."

"However," Chase said, "the phone company would have those records. They keep a copy of every text message sent."

"Seriously?" Sam said. I could tell she was mentally replaying the series of texts she and Kyle sent each other every night. "Do they read them?" Her cheeks turned a shade of bright crimson.

Chase shrugged. "Well, there isn't a guy sitting there going through every one, but they're stored. Usually for up to a week or two, until they need room to store the new ones."

"How do you know this?" I asked.

"The paper did a story on sexting a couple months back," he said. "Very illuminating." He winked at Sam.

She blanched.

"Okay, so assuming that the phone company does have a record of this text somewhere, what are the chances that they'll just hand it over to us?" I asked.

Chase reached across me and popped the rest of my entree in his mouth. "They won't. You need a warrant and probable cause to read someone's private texts."

Sam looked immensely relieved.

"Unless," Chase added.

"Unless?" Sam squeaked out.

"Unless you're one hell of a hacker." He grinned. A big toothy thing.

"I take that smug look to mean you know one hell of a hacker?" I asked.

"You're looking at him."

"Shut up," Sam said. "You can break into the phone company's computer?"

He shrugged. "Piece of cake. How do you think I got all those sexting messages?"

"You read them?" Sam asked.

He nodded. Then leaned in close. "You would not believe the filthy stuff some of our classmates are doing." He gave her another wink.

Sam looked like she was going to pass out from embarrassment.

"Let's go hack, then," I said.

"But I haven't had any lunch yet," Chase protested. Then he looked down at my salad. "You gonna eat that?"

Once Chase finished inhaling my lunch, we left the cafeteria and headed to the school library.

But we only got as far as the main wing when a frizzy-haired woman in a muumuu and Crocs stepped around the corner and almost slammed into me.

"Hartley!" she exclaimed. "I'm so glad I ran into you." She paused. "Literally," she added, then laughed at her own joke.

I gave her a blank look, racking my brain for who she

might be and why she might want to run into me, literally or otherwise.

"Mary Bessie," she helpfully supplied. "I'm the grief counselor."

Ah. Right. No wonder I didn't recognize her. I'd been avoiding her like the plague. The last thing I needed was to dissect the jumble of feelings I'd been doing a bang-up job of ignoring.

"Fab to meet you," I lied. "Unfortunately, I'm late for—"

But she didn't let me finish. "Listen, I'd love to schedule a time for us to talk." She punctuated this request by cocking her head to the right and doing an eyebrows-down, forehead-wrinkled, lips-pursed frown thing that was probably intended to be very sympathetic but mostly just made her look like she needed a Botox refresher.

"Oh, gee. That sounds like fun, Ms. Bessie—"

"Mary. Please." She did a big friendly grin at me. From the beige color of her teeth I pegged her as a coffee addict. Who didn't believe in Whitestrips.

"Okay. Mary. That's such a nice offer, but I'm good."

"Oh, honey." She tilted her head further. "I know you probably want to just pretend this whole thing didn't happen."

Boy, did I ever.

"But it's not healthy for you to bottle feelings up in

here," she said, gesturing to her torso. "You can't feel better unless you're willing to feel."

I felt Chase snort behind me.

"No, really. I'm fine. Nothing bottled."

"Okay." She put her hands up in a surrender motion. "It's not my place to push. Just know that I'm here"—she tilted her head even further, almost looking at me upside down—"when you're ready to let it out."

"Thanks. Yep. I'll definitely do that."

When hell froze over.

"Room twenty-five!" she called as I scuttled around her.

"Great!"

I made a mental note to find a route to trig that did *not* pass room twenty-five.

Five minutes later we were in the school library, staring at a row of state-of-the-art Macs. No matter how deeply the funding was cut, the computers in our school were always top-of-the-line and loaded with all the latest programs. And always Macs, courtesy of Wozniak's (the Apple cofounder) legacy as a philanthropist to our local education system. Philanthropy or clever advertisement, creating an entire generation of Mac users? Either way, I wasn't complaining as Chase sat down behind a screen and began typing in lines of code.

Silicon Valley is known as the technology hub of the world, spawning such companies as Apple, Google, and eBay, just to hit the biggies. Most kids who grow up here start using laptops as soon as they can hold their heads up. By three they're into online role-playing games. At ten they're writing their own programs, and by sixteen they're starting the beginnings of the next Apples and Googles. Or, in Chase's case, hacking into companies like Apple or Google.

Or Silicon Valley Wireless.

I watched as he pulled up the cell company's main website, clicking to the client log-in page.

"What's Courtney's phone number?" he asked.

I scrolled through my own phone until I hit her name in my address book. Not that I actually called Courtney Cline, but as any suspicious girlfriend knows, the first thing you do is check your boyfriend's phone for incoming calls from the other woman. The second I'd heard the rumors, I'd asked around for Courtney's number and branded it into my own phone for future snooping.

I rattled off the digits to Chase and watched him punch them into the web page. Then, instead of typing in Courtney's PIN, he opened another screen, typing a line of numbers and letters that meant nothing to me but must have meant something to the computer as it started spitting back its own lines of numbers and letters in response.

Ten minutes later I was starting to go cross-eyed from watching the little blinking cursor cruise across the screen.

"Are we there yet?" I whined.

"Almost" Chase said, never taking his eyes off the screen. "Patience, grasshopper."

Two agonizingly impatient minutes later, the screen changed, and Chase did a "yes" under his breath.

"You got it?" Sam asked.

He nodded. "We're in."

I knew I shouldn't be impressed by his criminal actions, but as the screen welcomed Courtney back to the site, I kinda was.

"So who sent her the text?" I asked.

"Hang on," Chase said, scrolling through a line of dates. He clicked on the day Courtney had died. A list of calls showed up.

A very long list.

"Holy shnikies, she was popular," Sam said.

I spun around.

"'Shnikies?'" I asked. "Someone catch a *Scooby-Doo* marathon lately?"

She stuck her tongue out at me. "Hey, you try censoring all the swear words out of your vocab and see how creative you get."

"She got exactly one hundred and fifty texts that day," Chase cut in.

Dude. Suddenly I felt unloved.

I turned back to the screen as Chase scrolled through the numbers, honing in on the ones time-stamped between when school got out and when we found her at Josh's place. Only fifteen fit the time frame.

And one fairly leaped out at me.

"There!" I stabbed my finger at the number on the screen next to the name J. DuPont. "That's Josh."

Chase clicked on it. The screen changed, the text of the message displayed. It was a one-liner:

my place. asap. c u there.

"So, he was lying." Chase sat back in his seat. I could swear I saw satisfaction glowing in his eyes.

But I shook my head. "Or he was telling the truth about someone setting him up. Isn't it possible someone borrowed his phone without him knowing?"

Chase shrugged. "You know him better than I do."

I bit my lip. Ninety percent of the time it took an act of God to pry Josh's cell from his person. But I knew of one time when he was most definitely phone free.

"Cross-country practice. Cody said he was there for a few minutes before he went home. He would have left his cell in his gym bag."

"Bingo," Sam said. "Someone could have totally grabbed his phone from his bag and sent the text. All it would take is a couple seconds."

"So, who had access to his gym bag?" Chase asked.

I shrugged. "The team leaves them next to the field while they practice. Anyone could have slipped it out for a minute and sent the text with no one being the wiser."

"Then we're back to square one," Sam said. She let out a sigh.

I leaned my chin on my elbow as I looked at the list of texts Courtney had received that day. Several came in from the usual suspects—Caitlyn, Kaylee, and various other Color Guard girls. A few were from names that I recognized as members of the football team. One from a T. Cline who I guessed was her mom. Some from people whose names sounded vaguely familiar.

And one that didn't seem to belong there at all.

"Check that out," I said, pointing to a text halfway through lunch period that day. It was from A. Brackenridge.

If Courtney had a polar opposite, Andi Brackenridge was it. For starters, she was a cheerleader, the natural antithesis of a Color Guard girl. And for another, Andi had gotten pregnant and missed spring semester last year when her baby girl was born. She was the embodiment of everything the Chastity Club stood against—an unwed teen mom who had worn her proof of sexual activity as a huge pregnant belly barely contained beneath her cheer uniform. The fact that she hadn't slunk off to be home-schooled or quietly obtained a GED with her tail between her legs had made her a prime target of the chastity crowd. After her boyfriend had dumped her in her third trimester, the Chastity Club had made Andi their virtual poster child for what happened to you if you didn't sign their Wait to Date pledge. Thanks in part to their merciless campaigning against her, Andi hadn't returned to school this year.

Which made her the last person I would expect to be sending chummy texts to Courtney.

"Click on this one," I directed, pointing at the screen.

Chase complied, the text displaying on the next screen.

i saw u. pay up bitch.

"Wow," Sam said. "Sounds like she was as much a fan of Courtney's as you were."

I elbowed her in the ribs.

"What did she see?" I wondered out loud.

And more important, had it gotten Courtney killed?

NINE

CHASE CLOSED THE BROWSER WINDOWS AND DELETED any evidence of our illegal snooping just as the warning bell rang, signaling the end of lunch. Sam hiked her backpack on her shoulder and took off for her lit class. I followed suit, enthusiastically heading to chemistry. And, no, the enthusiasm was not because I got off on memorizing the periodic table or anything. It was because both Kaylee and Caitlyn were in my class.

And I intended to grill them on all they knew about Courtney and Andi. They'd been quick to point the finger at Josh yesterday, but I wondered if there were other skeletons lurking in Courtney's closet they'd failed to mention.

I pushed through the doors to Mrs. Perry's class just as the final bell sounded, taking my usual place at a lab station in the third row. Caitlyn and Kaylee sat two stations up, front and center.

It wasn't until we'd all handed in our homework, Mrs. Perry had explained the day's experiment, and kids had split up into groups of two and three to try to follow the directions on the whiteboard while not blowing anything up that I got a chance to approach the perky pair.

Thing One and Thing Two had, predictably, partnered up for the experiment. Grabbing my book, I quickly made my way to the front of the room.

"Mind if I join your group?" I asked.

The look they shot me said they clearly *did* mind, but, lucky for me, good girls did not exclude other students. At least not within earshot of the teacher.

"Sure," Caitlyn said, loudly enough for Mrs. Perry to hear. "Happy to help you catch up."

She shot me a sugar-coated smile.

I matched it calorie for calorie.

"So," I said, pulling on a pair of rubber gloves and grabbing a test tube of bluish stuff. (Okay, I hadn't really been paying attention when Mrs. Perry explained what it was. I'd been too busy rehearsing how I'd casually bring up the subject of Courtney being threatened by Andi. A rehearsal I carefully put into practice . . .)

"I noticed a lot of people wearing those armbands," I said, pointing to the sparkly black accessory they each sported around their upper arms.

"Courtney was very popular," Caitlyn informed me.

Kaylee nodded solemnly. "Very."

"She had a lot of friends?"

Again, two blond heads bobbed in agreement. "Yes, tons," Kaylee said. "Though we were her *best* friends."

"Uh-huh," I said. "What about Andi Brackenridge? Was she a friend?"

Caitlyn scrunched up her nose like she'd smelled something foul. "Andi? God, what a loser. Andi was *definitely* not a friend of Courtney's," she told me, taking the bluish stuff from me and setting it ever so carefully in a wire holder.

"Huh. Well, that's odd."

"What?" Caitlyn asked. "What's odd?"

"That they weren't friends. Because Andi texted Courtney right before she died," I said, carefully watching their reactions.

But all I got was the I-just-smelled-rotten-meat nose scrunch.

"Who told you that?" Caitlyn demanded.

Excellent question.

"Uh . . . a friend. I'd tell you, but I can't divulge my sources." Nice. That sounded official.

"Well, they must be mistaken. No way would Courtney have anything to do with that skank," Caitlyn said definitively. Then she dropped a couple of white tablets into our blue mixture. It began bubbling. In spite of my preoccupation, I couldn't help noticing how cool it looked.

"Actually," I told her as I watched bubbles rise to the top of our test tube, "I saw the text message. It's no mistake."

"What kind of message?" Kaylee asked, biting her lip.

"A threat."

Kaylee's eyes went big and round. "Seriously?"

"Seriously," I said. "Andi said she saw Courtney and wanted her to pay up."

"Saw her doing what?" Kaylee asked. She shot a quick look at Caitlyn, but Thing One was carefully avoiding eye contact, instead focusing all her attention on sticking a straw into our bubbling brew and stirring.

"I was hoping maybe you knew."

Caitlyn shook her head, shampoo-commercial-shiny locks swishing against her shoulders. "Puh-lease. Andi is a complete lowlife. She's probably just making it up. You know she got pregnant when she was just *fifteen*," she said, emphasizing the word.

"What does that have to do with anything?"

"It shows her total lack of moral character."

I rolled my eyes. "Teenagers have sex, Caitlyn. Get over it."

"Well, they shouldn't," Caitlyn countered. "It's wrong. They should be saving themselves. Our bodies are our temples. They should have a little more respect for themselves than that."

"You know, I could have sworn I saw you shoveling Cheetos into your temple last week."

"Oh, but I'm pretty sure those were nonfat," Kaylee piped up.

Oh brother.

"Let's get back to Courtney," I said, steering the conversation before it disintegrated any further. (Which, by the way, is what was happening to our straw, the bubbling liquid eating away the plastic. What on earth was that blue stuff?) "Had Courtney mentioned being contacted by Andi lately?"

Caitlyn shook her head. "No. And Courtney told us everything. We were her best friends. Right, Kaylee?"

Kaylee looked down at the floor, nodded, and said in a voice that seemed for the first time to hold genuine sadness, "Yes, we were."

"Whatever Andi *thinks* she saw," Caitlyn continued, "she's clearly delusional. And there's no way Courtney would take a threat from her seriously anyway. I mean, Andi is a total loser. What could she possibly do to hurt Courtney?"

Beside strangle her with a pair of iPod earbuds? I wasn't sure.

But I was going to find out.

* * *

As soon as the final bell rang I headed for Sam's locker to tell her about my conversation with the Color Guard girls. Just my luck, Kyle had beaten me there and had Sam in a total lip-lock up against the lockers.

I cleared my throat, then looked away, trying to ignore the hollow feeling in the pit of my stomach that my own lips were now boyfriend free.

Sam looked up, extracted herself from Kyle, and blushed. "Hey, Hartley," she said.

Kyle turned around. "'Sup."

I waved, still feeling a little awkward as Kyle's hand rested on Sam's hip.

"So, I talked to Courtney's minions," I told Sam and relayed the conversation I'd had as the three of us walked through the halls.

"Do you believe them?" Sam asked, as we pushed through the doors and made our way down the front steps.

I shrugged. "They seemed genuinely surprised that Courtney would have anything to do with Andi."

"Dude, I remember Andi," Kyle cut in. "She was hot."

Sam punched him in the arm.

"Not as hot as you," he amended, rubbing at his bicep. "She's, like, a campfire, and you're totally a five alarm, babe."

Sam grinned. "Nice save."

Kyle leaned in and whispered something into Sam's ear. She giggled. I looked away, trying to ignore that hollow feeling again.

"There she is!" I heard someone call from across the front lawn.

I looked up to find Jessica Hanson pointing toward me. She was directing a vaguely familiar–looking woman dressed in a sharp gray suit, three layers of makeup, and spiky black heels that had her shifting from foot to foot to keep from sinking into the damp grass. Behind her stood a guy with a huge camera strapped to his waist and a pimply guy with a clipboard and the word *intern* fairly stamped on his forehead. And behind them, parked at the curb in front of the school, was a white KTVU News van with a satellite attached to the roof.

Oh boy.

"Hartley!" the woman called, charging forward with a black microphone in one hand.

I bit my lip and briefly contemplated escape, but it was a short-lived thought as the woman closed in, her entourage a step behind.

"Hartley Featherstone?" she asked. "Hi, I'm Diane Dancy from the KTVU Channel Two news. I was wondering if I could ask you a couple questions?"

"Umm . . . okay. I guess," I said, suddenly very conscious of the fact I hadn't looked in a mirror since fourth period. On instinct I raised a hand to my head, smoothing my hair down.

"Great," Diane said, gesturing to the camera guy.

He hoisted the camera up onto his shoulder and said, "In five, four, three . . ."

"Wait, you mean right now?" I asked, tucking more hair behind my ear, wishing she'd at least given me a chance to put on some lip gloss.

She ignored me, instead turning to the camera and whipping out the biggest smile I'd ever seen. "I'm Diane Dancy at Herbert Hoover High School where students are reacting to the gruesome murder of one of their own. I'm here with Hartley Featherstone, the student who found Courtney Cline's body. Hartley," she said, turning to me, "can you tell me how it felt to find your good friend murdered?"

"Uh . . . well, *good* is a strong word. . . ." I paused, looking from the microphone to the reporter to the little red light on the camera indicating that I was being broadcast to every home in the Bay Area.

"How did it feel when you realized she'd been murdered?" Diane pressed.

"It sucked?" I said. Only it came out more as a question.

"I'm sure it must have been incredibly traumatic for you."

Honestly? It kind of was. Despite the fact that Courtney

was not what I'd call a "good" friend, no one deserved to die like that. "It was," I answered, "but I'm sure it was much more traumatic for her."

"And you found her in your boyfriend's bedroom?"

"*Ex*-boyfriend," I clarified.

"Were you scared?"

"A little."

"Appalled?"

"Sorta."

"Fearful for your own life?"

"Um, well, not really—"

"Afraid that it could have been you?"

I narrowed my eyes. "What do you mean, it could have been me?"

"Do you believe it was luck that Josh snapped when he was with Courtney and not with you?"

"Wait—Josh did not snap."

"You mean you saw signs of his homicidal tendencies while you were dating?"

"No!" I held up my hand, shaking my head. "You have this all wrong. Josh is not a killer."

Diane gave me a skeptical look. "My sources within the law enforcement community have verified that he is a suspect."

"The police are wrong," I protested. "And—and we're going to prove it!"

She raised one artfully sculpted eyebrow. "We?"

"I'm working with the school's online paper, the *Herbert Hoover High Homepage,* to conduct an investigation."

I could see interest lighting behind Diane's eyes as she gestured to the camera guy to zoom in. "Tell me more about this investigation. What are you doing exactly?"

"Oh. Well . . ." I faltered, feeling the intensity of the camera on me. "We're, uh, looking at her classmates, friends, enemies—anyone who knew Courtney well. We've interviewed several people about her movements the day she was killed," I continued, gaining steam. "In fact, if anyone has information relating to Courtney's death, I urge them to contact me through the *Homepage*'s website."

"Has your investigation turned up anything interesting so far?" Diane asked.

I nodded. "Yes, it has, Diane. We have evidence that suggests someone other than Josh might have had a viable motive for killing Courtney."

"And what might that evidence be?" Diane pressed.

"Text messages."

"Where did you get these text messages?"

"Uh . . ." I figured it probably wouldn't be a great idea to admit to computer hacking on television. I glanced at Sam for help. She shrugged. "I'd rather not reveal my sources at this time."

Which sounded pretty weak even as I said it, but

apparently it was enough to convince Diane to drop it.

"Well, there you have it," she said, turning back to the camera. "Killer beware, because Herbert Hoover High has its very own Nancy Drew on the case."

Great. Just what I wanted to be known as.

As soon as the camera turned off, I grabbed Sam by the arm and hightailed it off campus before anyone else caught wind of the Nancy Drew comment. We speed walked the three blocks to her place where, ten minutes later, we were pleading our case to her brother to let us borrow the clean, green machine to track down Andi Brackenridge.

"Dude, again?" he asked from his position on the sofa. In front of him Animal Planet played on mute, and the coffee table at his side was littered with the remnants of both breakfast and lunch if the mix of cereal bowls, dried milk spills, and empty Chef Boyardee cans were any indication.

"Please, Kev?" Sam asked. "We're desperate."

"Can't you, like, take the bus? I'm low on fuel."

"We'll help you fill it up later," Sam said.

"Promise?"

"Cross my heart."

"Okay, I guess so," he finally said. "But bring me back a taco or something, 'kay? I'm starving."

We barely had time to nod before grabbing the keys and rushing out the door.

Ten minutes later we were driving the "Live Green!" advertisement down Union Avenue where, according to last year's school directory, Andi Brackenridge lived. We pulled up in front of a large, ranch-style place with a big square addition over the garage painted a shade of yellow just the slightest bit lighter than the rest of the house.

Sam shut the car off with a cough of French fry–scented smoke, and I followed her up the stone pathway to a white wooden front door. A welcome mat sat outside, and two potted begonias flanked the entryway. Sam knocked once, and two beats later we were greeted by a woman with long hair worn loose around her shoulders and streaked with highlights. She was dressed in a pair of skinny jeans, flip-flops with sparkles on the straps, and an Ed Hardy T-shirt. While she looked way too young to be a grandma, I recognized her from sixth grade Girl Scouts as Andi's mom.

"Mrs. Brackenridge?" I asked.

She nodded. "Can I help you?"

"We're looking for Andi. Is she in?"

She shook her head. "I'm sorry, she's working. Are you friends of hers?" she asked.

"We went to school with her," I said. Which was the truth, even if we hadn't spoken since middle school.

"Where does she work?" Sam asked.

"She sells Mary May cosmetics," Mrs. Brackenridge

responded. "You know, door-to-door."

That figured. The Andi I remembered from last year had been a virtual makeup addict—one more thing I guess Color Guard girls and cheerleaders had in common. Her signature color had been a combo of three different Bare Escentuals lipsticks with a glaze of Burt's Bees lip gloss over the top. I was pretty sure she took her makeup off each night with a chisel.

"Any idea where we can find her?" Sam pressed.

"She said she's working the Blossom Grove neighborhood today. Maybe you can catch her."

Blossom Grove was a planned community of single-family homes near the freeway. Big houses, small lots, spindly little trees tied to stakes amid square patches of lawn just big enough for a golden retriever to do his business.

We thanked Mrs. Brackenridge and climbed back into the Volvo, crossing our fingers that we had enough grease to make it.

After navigating through Orange Blossom Drive, toward Citrus Blossom Court, and down Blossom Breeze Avenue (Gee, think maybe someone had a thing for agriculture?), we finally spotted Andi in front of a large, two-story beige stucco house. While her hips were a little more generous than I remembered, there was no mistaking her dyed red hair and triple layer lips. She was wheeling a small, pink suitcase behind her and had a small, pink baby strapped to her chest in a snuggly carrier. Chubby little arms and legs were sticking out from her front like a starfish.

Sam pulled to a stop across the street.

"Hey, Andi!" I called as we got out.

She paused, putting one hand up to shield her eyes from the afternoon sun as she squinted at me.

"Do I know you?"

"Hartley Featherstone," I supplied, jogging across the street to meet her. "From Girl Scouts."

"Oh. Sure." Though I could tell from the blank look on her face she didn't really remember me. Or just didn't care.

"Listen, I'm glad we caught up with you. I wanted to ask you a couple questions."

Andi tilted her head to the side. "Questions? About makeup?" she asked. "Because we're running a special right now on moisturizing lip balms. Two for five bucks."

Hmmm, tempting . . .

"Actually, we were wondering if we could ask you about Courtney Cline."

Andi's face did a quick change from friendly saleswoman to PO'ed victim. "Courtney Cline was a total hypocrite, not to mention a complete bitch."

"I take it you weren't chummy?" I cleverly deduced.

"Chummy? Ha!" She tossed her hair over one shoulder, narrowly avoiding whipping the cooing baby in the face. "Look, I'm not gonna say anything bad about the dead—"

Too late.

"—but Courtney was definitely no friend of mine."

"The feeling is mutual," I said.

"I know. I heard the rumors."

Fanflippintastic. Did the whole town know?

The baby strapped to her front started to wiggle, causing Andi to rock from foot to foot. I had a feeling the little creature wasn't one for long conversations, so I got right to the point.

"We saw the text you sent Courtney on the day she died. The one where you threatened her."

Andi narrowed her eyes at me, sizing up my trustworthiness. Lucky for me, apparently our mutual dislike of all things Courtney did the trick.

"What about it?" she said. "I was offering her a little proposition."

"It looked like you were blackmailing her," Sam pointed out.

Andi shrugged it off. "Semantics."

"Tell me about the proposition," I said.

"Well . . ." She paused, looking over her shoulder as if the beige stucco might have ears. "I had proof that the chastity queen wasn't all she pretended to be."

"What kind of proof?"

"Video. Of her pulling a Paris Hilton, if you know what I mean."

A sick sensation bubbled up in my stomach, warning me that I shouldn't ask this next question. But somehow there was a disconnect between my brain and my mouth because it came out anyway.

"With who?"

Andi bit her lip, then gave me a sympathetic head tilt that was an exact duplicate of the grief counselor's. "Josh DuPont."

I concentrated very hard on breathing in and out for a full ten seconds before I trusted myself to speak.

"That craptastical, gutless, son-of-a-cactus-humping butt monkey!"

Maybe I should have taken twenty seconds.

"Sorry," Andi said. And she looked like she meant it. If anyone was acquainted with getting screwed over by a guy, it was her.

"Where did you get this video proof?" Sam asked, sending me a look from the corner of her eye as if she expected me to go postal any second. She knew me so well.

"I took it myself," Andi answered.

"Where? How?" I wished someone would fix that disconnect. Why did I keep asking questions I clearly did not want to hear the answers to?

The baby wiggled and Andi shifted on her feet again.

"Last Friday. I was at the football game, delivering some Very Cherry lip gloss to the cheer squad, when I saw Courtney and Josh head into the band room. I knew neither of them would touch a band geek with a ten-foot pole, so I figured I'd see what they were up to. That's when I caught them swapping bodily fluids behind the woodwind rack. Pretty sick, really."

Yep, I was totally going to throw up. "And you recorded it?"

Andi nodded. "I pulled out my phone and caught every filthy second."

"Let me see it." God, what was wrong with me?!

Andi bit her lip. "Are you sure that's a good idea?"

"Let. Me. See. It."

Andi turned to Sam. "You promise to hold her back if she freaks?"

Sam nodded. "I'll try."

"Okay," Andi agreed, pulling a pink phone from her back pocket. "But just remember—I'm only the videographer. So, like, don't shoot the messenger, right?"

I didn't answer, and instead focused on the tiny screen as the three of us crowded in to watch Andi scroll through thumbnails until she found one of the band room. She hit Play and leaned back, letting Sam and I squint at her phone.

The quality was suckish, grainy and really jerky as if

Andi couldn't hold still, and the sound was tinny. But there was no mistaking what was going on. I caught a naked leg, the flash of an iridescent purple Color Guard skirt sliding up a thigh, followed by the back of my boyfriend's head as he moved in for the kill. A few seconds later we heard moaning and panting.

I closed my eyes, shoving the phone away.

"I've seen enough." It was one thing to know your boyfriend had cheated, but entirely another to actually see it.

God, I felt so stupid.

"You okay?" Sam gently asked.

No. "Yeah."

"It's pretty clear what was going on," Andi said, pointing to the video.

"Crystal."

"Anyway, after all the crap that Courtney put me through, I couldn't wait to expose her for the hypocrite she was."

"But you didn't expose her," Sam pointed out.

Andi shook her head. "No. When I got home and saw the footage, I had a better idea. As you can imagine, I'm a little short on cash these days. Do you have any idea how much a baby costs?" she asked.

Sam and I both shook our heads.

"A million dollars."

I blinked. Then looked down at the seemingly innocent

little pink bundle in her pouch.

"I know, right?" Andi said. "But analysts say that a baby born this year will cost its parents more than a million dollars over the course of their lifetime. I don't have that kind of money. So, I had a better idea than calling Courtney out."

"You decided to blackmail her."

She nodded. "I sent her a few choice moments of the footage I shot and told her that if she didn't buy me diapers for a year, it would end up all over YouTube."

My stomach roiled again at the thought of proof of my boyfriend's cheating plastered all over the internet.

"What did she say?" Sam asked.

"She said she'd pay. Only she died before we could discuss specific terms." Andi did a wistful sigh, looking down at her baby. "Too bad."

"Where were you when she was killed?" Sam asked.

Andi's eyes shot up. "What do you mean?"

"Do you have an alibi?"

I rolled my eyes at the term. Diane Dancy was right. We did sound Nancy Drew. But I had to admit I was curious, too.

"Wait—you don't think I had anything to do with her death, do you?"

Sam shrugged. "Did you?"

"No! God, no. Why would I want her dead?"

"You weren't exactly her biggest fan," I pointed out.

"Neither were you."

Good point.

"You didn't answer the question," Sam pressed.

Andi put her hands on her hips. "I was at the doctor's, okay? Chloe had her six-month checkup. You can ask anyone there if you don't believe me. She screamed bloody murder when she got her shots. Besides," she continued, "if anything, I had every reason to want Courtney alive. Check it—I'm out a year's supply of diapers because some guy offed her before I could get my due. No way I did this."

Andi had a point. On *Law & Order* it was always the blackmailer not the blackmailee that ended up dead. And it didn't seem like Andi had much of a motive to kill her.

"Now, unless you're going to buy something, I have work to do," Andi said, gesturing to her suitcase.

I paused. "You still have cherry lip gloss left?"

She nodded.

"I'll take two."

TEN

THE SECOND WE GOT BACK TO THE GREEN MACHINE, I grabbed Sam's phone and sent an urgent message to Josh's MySpace account.

Need to c u. 2nite. Window will b open.

Then I spent the rest of the drive back to my place slowly counting to ten, cursing Josh in the most creative way I knew how, then counting to ten again.

"Wow, you know a lot of swear words," Sam commented at one point. "And here I thought I had a dirty mouth."

"What can I say? Apparently candid porn starring my boyfriend brings out the best in me."

"I always knew he was an effing jerk."

"Thanks." I appreciated her show of support, censored as it might be.

By the time Sam dropped me off in front of my place, I had almost gotten my roiling stomach under control.

Almost.

Then I saw Detective Raley's car sitting at the curb.

I took two deep breaths, counted to twenty this time, then walked up to the driver's-side window of his sedan. It rolled down to reveal the detective himself.

"Good afternoon, Miss Featherstone," he said.

"It would be."

He raised an eyebrow. "If?"

"If you were looking for the real killer instead of staking me out." A ballsy statement. Apparently pervy videos also brought out my honest side.

Unfortunately Raley was way too much of a cool customer to be jarred by my honesty.

"Trust me, Miss Featherstone, our department is using every resource to locate Courtney's killer. We will find him." The way he stared straight at me as he said it made it sound more like a threat than a reassurance.

"Which reminds me," he went on. "Seen Josh today?"

I shook my head. "Nope."

"Well, I guess I'll just wait here for a bit and see if he shows up."

"Great. Have fun with that," I said with the most sarcasm I could muster. Which was a lot.

While I wasn't thrilled with the idea of Raley basically

cop stalking me at any time, today it was especially annoying. Because as soon as Josh arrived, I planned on killing him. And I didn't particularly want Raley as a witness.

The minute I walked in the door the aroma of homemade lasagna greeted me, signaling that instead of going to her usual water aerobics class, Mom had opted to work out her anxiety through comfort food again. I had to admit, it did smell kind of good. And I could use a little comfort. Even if it was made of gluten-free noodles and seasoned ground tofu.

Once I'd devoured two big slices, I escaped the grasp of the SMother and headed to my room. I immediately opened my window, checking outside to make sure Josh had a clear path. The last thing I wanted was for him to get hurt on his way to me killing him.

Once I was sure he could arrive for his death unharmed, I halfheartedly did my homework, then flipped on the TV and watched *American Idol* while keeping one eye on the window. Then watched an episode of *Castle* On Demand. Then the late news, where Diane showed my clip (wow, I *really* wish she'd let me pause for lip gloss) and told the Bay Area that while there was still no break in the case of the "Herbert Hoover High killer," the other members of the Chastity Club were starting a Courtney Cline Memorial Fund to help spread the message of teen abstinence.

I was just slipping on a pair of sweats and crawling into bed, resigned to the idea that Josh had somehow been tipped off to his ultimate doom and chickened out, when I heard a sound outside. Like a squirrel. A really big one.

I ran to the window and saw Josh shimmying up the tree outside. He braced himself on the trunk with his Converses, then swung onto a low-hanging branch like Tarzan. He spotted me, gave a little wave, then scooted out along the branch until he was flush with my windowsill. I stepped back as he lifted one foot, then the other over the sill and fell with a grunt onto my floor.

"Hey," he said, standing up. He brushed his palms on the seat of his jeans. "Sorry it took me awhile. There's a car parked in front of your house."

I crossed to the window on the other side of the room, looking out over the roof toward the street beyond. I could just make out the front fender of Raley's nondescript sedan.

"That's Raley."

"Who?"

"The detective who wants to 'question' you."

"Oh." Josh's face paled a shade.

"He didn't see you, did he?" I asked, taking another glance at the unmarked car.

Josh shook his head. "I cut through the neighbor's yard at the back."

"That's the first smart thing you've done," I said.

Josh's eyes immediately registered hurt.

I expected to feel satisfied or vindicated by hurting him. But I didn't. I just felt worse. How come he could be a jerk, but when I was a jerk, stupid guilt took all the fun out of it?

"I deserve that," he admitted. "And I'm sorry for dragging you into this, Hartley," he said, taking a step toward me.

I took one back.

The last thing I wanted Josh DuPont to be was sorry. I wanted him to be a creep, a jerk, the cheating turd that I now knew without a doubt he was. If he felt sorry, it meant he had a conscience, had feelings. Possibly even for me. Possibly ones I would be tempted to return. And I didn't want to return them. Last spring my grandma Betty had passed away. It had been really sudden. One day she was fine, the next she went to the doctor for what we thought was a routine checkup and came out with a diagnosis of stage four stomach cancer. Two weeks later she passed away in her sleep. I'd been devastated.

Josh and I had only just started dating at that point, but he had been my rock. He'd held my hand, passed me the tissues, and even gone with me to her funeral. Not once had he flashed that slightly pained look most guys get when the tears come out. Instead, he'd said, "It's going to be okay," and gave me the same soft, understanding, compassionate pair of blue eyes he was currently sending me. Ones that said he understood how I felt and wished he could make it better.

Only this time, there was no making it better.

I took a deep breath, conjured up the mental image of that band room video, and reminded myself why I had asked Josh here.

"I have a witness."

He cocked his head. "A witness to what?"

"You and Courtney. She has video."

He paused. "Video of what?"

"What do you think?"

He was smart enough not to answer. Instead, he said, "I didn't kill her."

"But you slept with her."

"I—" he started.

But I didn't let him finish. "Don't even try denying it. I *saw* you, Josh. God, how could you?"

He took another step toward me. "Hartley, I'm so sorry—"

"Don't you dare be sorry!"

He froze.

"Look, it's not like I wanted things to happen this way, Hartley."

"How exactly did you want them to happen, Josh?" I asked, my voice rising. "Behind my back?"

"No." But I could tell that was exactly how he'd wanted them to happen. "I didn't mean to hurt you."

"No, you didn't mean for me to find out."

"It's not like that."

"Then tell me, Josh, exactly what is it like?"

He looked down at the floor. "We were at a football game in Walnut Creek. It was after the meet, we'd just won, and we were coming back home on the bus. Courtney sat next to me, and one thing led to another . . ."

"I do not want to hear this." A truer phrase I have never uttered.

"It just happened."

"Earthquakes just happen. Tornadoes just happen. Your tongue does not just happen to fall into some other girl's mouth!" Not to mention certain other body parts that I was *not* going to think about.

Josh bit his lip. "I'm sorry," he said for the gazillionth time.

I should have backed away then, licked my wounds, let my pride begin the slow process of recovery. Instead, I asked, "Why?" Because, clearly, I am some sort of masochist.

"Why am I sorry?"

"Why did you sleep with the president of the Chastity Club?!"

He took a deep breath. "Okay, you wanna know the truth?"

"No, I'd prefer to continue hearing the lies fall out of your mouth."

He sighed, then looked down at the floor. "Look, you and I have been dating for six months, Hartley. Six months. Face it, you were never gonna give it up."

Oh, he did *not* just say that.

I don't know what I'd hoped to hear. Maybe that Courtney was prettier than me, smarter than me, better at crossword puzzles.

But what it came down to was that the chastity queen put out and I didn't.

"Seriously? That's your reason? You cheated on me with Courtney Cline—Courtney Cline of all people!—because I wouldn't sleep with you?"

"I respect that you're a virgin," Josh said, "but, Hartley, come on."

"Come on? Come on?! That's the best you can do?" My entire relationship with my first true love had come down to two little words.

"I'm sorry."

I felt hot tears backing up behind my eyes but refused to give him the satisfaction of shedding even one.

"You are such a jerk."

"It didn't mean anything."

"It meant something to me."

"Hartley—"

He reached out a hand toward me.

"Don't you dare touch me. You do not get to touch me. Just go."

He opened his mouth to speak but must have thought better of it.

"I'm sorry," he said again. Then he turned and slipped out the window the way he'd come.

I had the fleeting idea to run out front and tell Detective Raley just where he could find Josh DuPont. I had the feeling I'd find immense satisfaction in seeing him haul my ex-boyfriend away in handcuffs. I might even help them beat a confession out of him.

But the truth was, even through my anger, I knew Josh hadn't killed Courtney. He was a weasel of the lowest order. Which just served to solidify my theory that he didn't have the guts to kill Courtney.

So who did?

ELEVEN

I SPENT THE REST OF THE NIGHT ALTERNATING BETWEEN crying, punching my pillows in lieu of Josh's face, and whining to Sam on the phone. Good friend that she was, not only did she let me keep her up way too late, she ditched the censoring thing long enough to call him a string of names that would have made a sailor blush.

"Thanks, I needed that," I told her.

"No prob." She paused. "So, you're totally through with him, right?"

I nodded at the phone. Then said, "I didn't call him quite as creative names as you just did, but, yeah, I am. Totally over him."

I'm proud to say I actually finished that sentence before bursting into tears. Luckily, Sam had unlimited minutes and didn't mind hearing me blubber incoherently about just how over Josh I was late into the night.

I awoke the next morning groggy, puffy eyed, and generally feeling like I'd been hit by a truck. A big one. That had backed up, hit me again, then shown me a video of my boyfriend doing a perky brunette.

I brushed my teeth twice, trying to get the bad taste of Josh's confession out of my mouth, washed my face with an apricot scrub that left my skin raw and tingly, then tied my hair back into a no-nonsense ponytail, ready to face the day.

As an eff-you to my crappy mood I put on a pair of skinny jeans, some sparkly silver flats, and a loose T-shirt with silver sequins all over. I capped it off with pair of silver earrings, hoping the dangling hoops would distract from my red-rimmed eyes. Then I added a layer of mascara and eyeliner just to be sure.

I grabbed my book bag and managed to slip out the front door before Mom could shove a bowl of oatmeal with agave syrup at me, instead walking the two blocks over to the nearest Starbucks and ordering a venti latte. Double shot.

By the time I walked the rest of the way to school, I was caffeinated, renewed, and ready to start my day.

Unfortunately, the first person I saw was Mary Bessie, grief counselor extraordinaire.

"Hartley!"

"Hi, Ms. Bessie."

"Mary. How are you, Hartley?"

"Fine." I loved that word. It covered all manner of sins. No matter the situation, one could always feign fineness.

"You look like you've been crying," she said, doing her patented head tilt as she scrutinized my eyes.

So much for CoverGirl.

"I'm fine."

"You sure?"

"Very."

"I'm here if you want to talk about how you're feeling right now. You know, tears are emotion in motion."

I did a mental eye roll. "I'm late for English."

"The warning bell hasn't even rung yet."

"Nice chatting with you," I called, backing away.

She stood in the doorway to her office, her head still tilted, annoying sympathy oozing from her polyester-clad frame.

I managed to make it through lit and the next two periods without incident. Today, the sidelong glances from my peers were fewer and farther between, the chatter continuing as I passed instead of immediately ceasing with a hissed, "It's her!" It had been two whole days since Courtney had been found dead. An eternity. I thanked God for the short attention span that had been electronically bred into my generation. At this rate, by the end of the week no one would remember Courtney at all, let alone the poor clue-less chick whose boyfriend had effed her, allegedly killed her, and left her for said chick to find.

In fact, by fourth period, I'd almost forgotten it myself.

It wasn't until lunch that I was ripped away from my BFF, denial, again.

"Hey, Hart."

I looked up from my locker to find Chase bearing down on me. He was doing the black-on-denim thing again, his hair looking slightly more spiky than usual, as if he'd spent the morning running his hands through it. In frustration, if the concerned line of his eyebrows was any indication.

"I need to talk to you," he said.

"So talk," I said, shoving my chem book into my bag.

He looked past me at the crowded hallway, then low-ered his voice. "An anonymous tip came in to the paper. About Courtney."

I raised one eyebrow. "Anonymous tip? That seems a little melodramatic, doesn't it?"

"If you like that, you'll love this. It's from someone who referred to himself as 'Deep Blogger.' He says he saw who killed Courtney Cline."

"Really?" I asked, skepticism lacing my voice.

"Really."

"So who killed her?" I asked.

"I don't know. He didn't say."

"Of course he didn't."

"He said he'd only tell you."

"Me?!"

"Shhhh!"

I lowered my voice. "Why me?"

Chase shrugged. "I guess he saw your TV interview."

"Fine. Give him my email addy."

But Chase shook his head. "He said he couldn't risk sending that sort of information via email. He wants to meet with you in person."

"That's just wonderful." I threw my hands up.

"It gets better. He said he'd be on the football field. At midnight tonight. And you should come alone."

I rolled my eyes. "Seriously? Am I living in an episode of *CSI: Silicon Valley*?"

Chase grinned. "Cute."

Despite my foul mood, I think I blushed. "I was going for exasperated, not cute."

"Try harder next time," he said, still grinning. A dimple dented his left cheek, totally at odds with the Danger: Bad Boy Ahead image he was cultivating.

"*Anyway*," I said, "this feels like a total prank. Midnight? Come alone?"

"My thoughts exactly."

I blew out a puff of air, ruffling my hair. "I am so sick of this. I swear if I get out there and no one shows up . . ."

"Whoa. Wait—you're not actually thinking of meeting him, are you?"

I turned to him. "Of course. I mean, it's probably a prank, but I need to be sure, right?"

"No!" he shouted.

"Shhh!" I said, turning the tables on him.

He failed to see the irony, completely ignoring me as he continued. "No, I definitely do *not* think you should meet him."

"Why not?"

"Didn't we just go over this? Alone? In the middle of the night? In a deserted location?"

I put my hands on my hips. "The HHH football field is hardly the middle of nowhere. I think I'll be okay, *Mom*."

But he shook his head again. "No. No way can I let you go."

"I'm sorry, 'let me'? Since when did you become my keeper?"

"Hartley, we're dealing with a killer here. This is not some game."

"Oh, gee, I'm sorry. Here I thought we were playing Parcheesi."

Again, my excellent sarcastic wit was wasted on him.

"I'll go," he said.

"And that's safer because?"

"I'm a guy."

"Right, and having a pair of dingle balls makes you invincible how?"

"Okay, now you're just being unreasonable."

I threw my hands up. "In the past two days I've been cheated on, lied to, stalked by both a cop and a grief counselor, and now, thanks to an overzealous reporter, the entire student body thinks I'm some sort of wannabe Nancy Drew, and I've got a date with a secret informant on a damp field in the middle of the night. I think I've earned the right to be a little unreasonable!"

"You are not meeting this guy."

"I'm *so* meeting him."

"I don't like this, Hartley."

"I don't care what you like!"

He narrowed his eyes at me. "Hey, what's with the attitude? I'm not the one you should be pissed at here."

He was right. I was totally projecting. I was pissed at Josh, but Chase was a closer target. And the whole macho thing was not winning him any points today.

"I'm just looking out for your well-being," Chase said. "I don't want you to get hurt."

"Why does everyone say that when what they really mean is that they don't want to feel guilty?"

"That's not what I mean."

"Whatever."

Chase shook his head. "Why are you even doing this?"

"Arguing with you? Good question. You're really not worth the time."

"No. Trying to help Josh. The guy who *cheated* on you."

I felt my face flush, my cheeks burning. "I know he cheated. Don't you think I know that?"

"Then why do you still care?"

"I don't!"

"I don't believe you."

"I don't care what you believe."

Chase threw his hands up. "You know what? Fine. Go meet this psycho killer on the football field at midnight. Knock yourself out!"

"Fine. I will!"

"Good!"

"Great!"

By this point our conversation had escalated into a bona fide shouting match. Every head within eyeshot was turned our way. Chris Fret stood at his locker, his hands frozen over a cross-country jersey, his mouth open. Jessica Hanson was filming us on her phone. The Color Guard girls were openly staring, Caitlyn narrowing her eyes at us, while Kaylee chewed on a fingernail, looking concerned.

I slammed my locker shut and ducked my head, turning my back on Chase as I stalked off.

God, I hated guys.

* * *

I hid out in the girls' bathroom for the rest of lunch period, then kept my nose glued to my books through chem and trig. As soon as the last bell sounded I sprinted for the doors, managing to sneak away with only a few ill-concealed glances from the curious. Needless to say, by that time every person at HHH with a cell phone knew about my fight with Chase. In fact, one text had even been mistakenly sent to me:

hart's totally lost it.

I texted back that Cody ought to check his contacts more carefully before sending mass messages.

oops. Srry.

I ignored the apology—I'd had enough of those to last me a lifetime—and made my way home.

Of course Raley was once again parked in front of my house. I was beginning to think of him as a permanent fixture. Kinda like a big, annoying garden gnome.

"Caught any bad guys today?" I asked as I walked past.

He just shook his head and retaliated with, "Nope. Seen Josh today?"

"Nope."

Neither of us believed that, but I didn't give him a chance to question me any further, quickly heading up the walkway.

I stuck my key in the lock and opened the door to find a note from Mom taped to the entry credenza:

Went to Spin class. Cake in the fridge. Love you.

Cake. Some days I loved my mom. I went straight to the fridge and pulled out a chocolate thing dripping with icing. Okay, so it was made with chickpea flour and carob frosting. But, really, there wasn't much you could do to ruin chocolate cake. I cut myself a huge slice, then dug into the freezer for my secret stash. There was half a pint of Chunky Monkey left. I scooped it on top of the cake, then sat at the counter and savored every decadent bite.

After I had completely gorged myself, I trudged up to my bedroom, turned on MTV, and pulled out my trig book. How was it fair that I had to conduct a murder investigation *and* do trig? All Raley did was sit outside my house in his sedan, no doubt downing donuts.

Several deliciously dramatic reality shows later, I heard Mom's minivan pull into the driveway, followed closely by a knock at my door.

"Hart? You there?" Mom asked as she peeked her head into my room.

I did a little wave from my cross-legged position on my bed. "Hey."

"Homework done?"

"Yep."

"You get something to eat?"

"Yep."

"You doing okay?"

"Yep."

"Got everything you need?"

"Yep."

"Okay . . ." Mom lingered in the doorway even though she'd clearly run out of questions to ask.

"Well . . . have a good night, then," she finally said.

"Thanks." I paused, then added, "you, too," feeling just the teensiest bit guilty about lying to her after she made me a cake.

Okay, I guess technically I wasn't lying. But I certainly hadn't felt compelled to tell her that I was planning to slip out to meet an anonymous witness at midnight in the deserted football field.

Then again, considering such information was likely to give her a heart attack, I was actually being a pretty good daughter by lying.

I looked up at the clock. 11:30 p.m. It was now or never.

TWELVE

I PULLED ON A PAIR OF BLACK STRETCH PANTS, A BLACK hoodie, and my sneakers, just in case there was anything lurking out there to run away from. I looked out the front window. Raley was still parked at the curb, his fender just visible from my vantage point. No doubt his beady little eyes were trained on my front door as if Josh might magically appear at any second.

Unfortunately, I didn't think he'd miss me slipping out of said door, either.

I turned around and looked to my back window. If Josh could climb in, surely I could climb out, right?

I crossed the room, lifted the window open, and looked down.

That ground looked awfully hard and awfully far away.

I hesitated a brief moment, wondering if it was too

late to call Chase and take him up on his offer to meet Deep Blogger. But that meant swallowing my pride and admitting I was a chicken. I'd had my ego bruised one too many times already in the past week. I wasn't sure it could recover from another hit.

So, despite my better judgment, I took a deep breath, stepped over the sill, and leaned toward the oak tree that Josh had used to climb in my room. I experienced just the slightest tinge of vertigo as my foot hung suspended in air over the two-story drop.

Be cool, Hart. Be cool.

I took another deep breath and leaned to the right, stretching my foot as far as I could. The tip of my Nikes touched the largest branch. I let go of the sill with one hand, again stretching toward the tree, channeling Mom's yoga obsessions. I got one foot on, but it was hardly a stable foothold. I was gonna have to jump for it.

I closed my eyes, said a silent prayer, and held my breath. I could do this. I was monkey girl. I would not fall.

I pulled my leg back onto the sill, kneeling in the opening. Then I swung my arms and jumped.

For one terrifying moment, I was suspended in air above our crabgrassy lawn. Then my hands connected with the tree branch, and I clamped on like my life depended on it (which, at this point, it did). I gave myself a two count to collect my strength again, then shimmied down the branch, feetfirst, toward the center of the tree where the limbs converged.

The second my feet hit the trunk, I let out a sigh of relief so loud, I was sure Raley heard me out front. I crouched down in the dark, listening with my entire body to the sounds of the suburban night: a TV in my neighbor's bedroom spouting canned laughter, a cat yowling down the street, a dishwasher humming contentedly from the house behind mine.

But no nosy detectives.

So far, so good.

I wrapped my arms around the trunk, slowly easing myself downward, then dropped the last few feet to the ground. I slunk around the tree, keeping to the shadows and out of range of the motion-detecting lights on our back patio, until I reached the side yard. Careful to avoid the garbage cans, I undid the latch on the back gate and peeked out.

Raley was still parked in the same spot out front, eyes glued to the front door.

In the immortal words of Mr. Burns . . . eeeeeeexcellent.

I quickly slipped out the gate, latching it behind me, then ducked my head and took off toward school.

It was only about a ten-minute walk to the football field, but I felt like a fugitive the entire way, ducking the big bad law stationed on my street.

I was shivering from the cold by the time I hit the school. I pulled my sleeves down over my hands, wishing I'd brought my down coat. But it was white. Not exactly stealth colored.

Blowing out visible puffs of air, I skirted around the front of the school. It was originally built at the beginning of the last century, all tall columns, tons of white concrete, and large imposing steps up to the front doors. Lit from below with strategically placed lights, it looked like a giant mausoleum in the night.

Not that my imagination was running away with me or anything.

I wrapped my arms around myself, trying not to play any particular horror movie scenes in my head as I speed walked the length of the building, crossed the back parking lot, and hit the quiet, dewy football field.

Deep Blogger had said specifically in the email Chase forwarded to me that he would meet me beneath the back bleachers. I blinked in the darkness, trying to get my bearings as I entered the first row of seats.

I took three steps, then thought I heard a sound to my left and quickly swung around. I squinted through the nothingness.

"Hello?" I called out.

No response.

I swallowed a gulp of cowardice, quickening my pace toward the last row.

Where I was sure I heard a sound this time.

"Hello?" I called again. "Deep Blogger?" I felt kinda ridiculous calling out his pseudonym, but "Hey, mysterious informant!" felt just as silly.

There was a pause. Then a raspy voice answered back. "Are you alone?"

I was surprised to hear it was female, though I could tell she was taking pains to disguise it by adding a fake rasp. Because I would recognize it? I took a step forward, trying to make out the owner, but all I could see was the faint outline of a person. It looked like she was dressed all in black, a hoodie pulled up over her head. She could have been Heidi Klum or the Unabomber for all I could tell.

"Yes," I answered. "I'm alone."

"Are you armed?"

I rolled my eyes. "No. Why would I be armed?"

"Turn around so I can see you."

I held my arms out and did an exaggerated spin for my dramatic informant's viewing pleasure.

"Satisfied?" I asked.

I saw the form nod.

Good. Time to get down to business.

"You saw who killed Courtney Cline?" I asked.

"I did."

I paused, waiting for her to go on. When she didn't, I prompted, "Well? Who was it?"

"First I need some assurance that I'll be safe."

"Like what?"

"You'll protect my identity."

"Well, considering I have no idea who you are, that shouldn't be a problem. How do you know who killed Courtney?"

"I saw the killer."

"How?" I asked.

"I was outside Josh's house when Courtney was killed. I saw the killer go inside."

I bit my lip. "Okay, I'll bite—who did you see?"

"I'll tell you." The shadow took a step closer, coming toward me. "It was . . ."

The voice faltered. I heard a sound like feet tripping over each other on the grass. There was a sharp intake of air and a second later a high-pitched yelp.

Then I watched in horror as my best lead yet turned and began to run in the opposite direction.

"Wait!" I shouted, turning after her. "Don't go!"

But Deep Blogger didn't pay any attention, taking off at a full sprint toward the parking lot.

I ducked my head and ran after her.

Only I didn't get far.

As I passed the spot where she'd been standing in the

shadows, I felt myself trip over something on the ground, my left foot catching as I slipped forward.

I threw my hands out in front of me to break my fall, my palms sliding on the wet grass.

I craned my head back to see what I'd stumbled on.

And that's when I heard a new sound. A long, loud scream, echoing eerily off the abandoned metal bleachers.

It took me a minute to realize it was coming from me, as my entire being was focused on the object on the ground that, incidentally, my left foot was still caught under.

Kaylee Clark lay on the grass, her legs twisted under her body, her vacant eyes staring blankly into the starry sky, a dark pool of blood under her head.

THIRTEEN

I QUICKLY PULLED MY FOOT OUT FROM UNDER KAYLEE AND scrambled to my feet. Or tried to. I tripped, falling on the ground again, wet mud squishing between my fingers. It felt like it took an eternity for me to find my feet a second time and actually make them move in the opposite direction of the body. When I finally did, I took off running, my body moving without any input from my brain. Which was a good thing, because at present the only thing my brain could do was chant, "ohmigod, ohmigod, ohmigod" over and over again. I ran blindly through the dark, making it to midfield before I ran into a solid wall.

"Whoa." Hands went around my upper arms, holding me still.

"Rape!" I screamed instinctively, swatting at my attacker. It was far from the truth, but as a girl it was what

I'd been programmed to yell when attacked. I smacked in the general direction of his face.

"Hartley!" His head jerked back, but his hold stayed strong.

I paused. I recognized that voice.

"Jesus, calm down."

Let me tell you, I had never been so glad to see that overweight, redheaded cop in my life.

"Ohmigod, ohmigod! Kaylee. Over there. Ohmigod!"

"Calm down," Detective Raley said again. "Take a breath."

I did, dragging in cold air that burned my lungs. "Kaylee Clark. She's"—I took another breath—"dead."

In the shadows, I could see Raley's eyebrows hunkering down, making his forehead a mass of wrinkles.

"Show me."

While the last thing I wanted to do was go back to where I knew Kaylee was bleeding beneath the bleachers, the tone of Raley's voice broached no argument. So, I did.

My feet refused to move any farther as soon as the bleachers came into view again, so I pointed a straight arm (okay, a slightly trembling arm) toward the last row.

"There."

Raley nodded. "Stay here."

Yeah, like I was going anywhere.

I watched Raley approach the inert object under the

bleachers. I saw him crouch down, examining Kaylee closer, then straighten back up and pull out his cell. I was too far away to hear more than a muffled conversation, but I could well imagine what he was saying. I'm pretty sure the word "coroner" was involved.

I hugged my arms around myself, the chill biting despite the sweat I'd broken into at the first sight of Kaylee. I looked down at my feet. A big, red smear covered the toe of my white Nikes. I told myself it wasn't blood. Probably just ketchup I'd dropped during lunch. Maybe nail polish I'd spilled at some point. Definitely not blood, and definitely not from a dead girl. I forced my eyes up, making myself promise never to look at my feet again.

Raley walked back over to me, a grim expression on his face.

"She's dead."

Even though I knew that had been coming, I felt my stomach roll. Another dead body at Herbert Hoover High.

And found by me.

A sick sense of déjà vu hit as I watched the CSU crawl across the football field. The area was lit up now by the huge floodlights circling the stadium. Uniformed officers staggered every four feet made a human chain, scanning the grass for evidence. The coroner and a handful of other guys in cheap suits knelt over poor Kaylee's body. And

Raley stood in front of me, feet planted shoulder width apart, his notebook out, grilling me like a summer hamburger. Apparently I hadn't been quite as stealthy as I'd thought, as Raley had, in fact, seen me slipping down the street and decided to follow me. Though, at the moment, I couldn't be too upset that he had. If he hadn't stopped me, I'd probably still be running through the night, fueled by pure adrenaline.

"So, what were you doing out here?" he asked, pen hovering.

"I told you. I was meeting Deep Blogger."

He raised an eyebrow at me. "And who is this 'Deep Blogger'?" he asked, doing air quotes around the name as if he didn't quite believe me.

"I don't know. That's the whole point of her being Deep Blogger. It's an alias."

"Yeah. I got that." He looked down at his notes. "You don't have a name?"

"No."

"But you said, 'her.' You know it's a girl?"

I looked down at my feet. Bad idea. The Smear stared me in the face. I quickly raised my eyes to meet Raley's. "The voice was female. That's all I know."

"And you think this Deep Blogger killed Kaylee?"

"Yes. No. Maybe."

Again with the raised eyebrow.

I took a deep breath. "Look, I don't know. I was meeting her here, and all of a sudden she just turned around and ran."

"And why were you meeting her?"

I bit my lip. As much as I knew it wasn't the wisest decision of my life to lie to the police, especially when dealing with a double homicide, I had promised Deep Blogger that I'd keep her identity as a witness safe. Not that she'd actually had time to tell me what she'd witnessed, but tipping my hand to Raley wasn't going to help that any.

"Hartley?" Raley prompted.

"There was a tip," I finally said.

"What kind of tip?"

"An anonymous one."

He narrowed his eyes at me. "From who?"

I threw my arms up. "Well, if I knew that, it wouldn't be very anonymous, would it?"

He narrowed his eyes at me. "Look, Hartley, the police get 'anonymous tips,'" he said, again doing the air quotes with his fingers. "Teenagers do not."

"Okay. Fine. You follow your tips and I'll follow mine."

"You're not being very cooperative, Miss Featherstone."

"I know."

Raley pursed his lips so hard they all but disappeared. "How did you get this tip?"

"It came in to the school paper."

"And what did the tipster say?"

"I can't tell you."

"Why?"

"Journalistic integrity."

"You are not a journalist."

"I am now," I said, pulling myself up to my full height. "The *HHH Homepage* has partnered with me to investigate Courtney's death. Something you'd know if you'd watched the news last night instead of my front door."

Raley put a hand to his forehead, massaging the spot between his eyes as if I was giving him a headache.

Ditto here, pal.

"Okay, let's go back to tonight," he said. "You met with this blogger, then what happened?"

"I told you. She took off."

"Any idea why?"

I shrugged. "My best guess? She found Kaylee just like I did."

"Yes, interesting that."

My turn to narrow my eyes. "What do you mean?"

"You finding a dead body. Again."

"What are you saying?"

"Nothing." Raley looked down at his notes, effectively obscuring his expression. "Just . . . interesting."

"Do I need a lawyer here?" I asked.

Raley looked up, his eyes squarely meeting mine. "I don't know. Do you?"

I crossed my arms over my chest, exercising my right to remain silent.

"When was the last time you saw Josh?" Raley asked, jumping on his favorite go-to question as if asking it enough times might break me down.

Luckily, I was saved from answering by a voice hailing me from across the field.

"Hartley!" I turned and saw Mom flying at me with a speed that would make the HHH football coach sign her up on the spot. "Oh, my baby," she cried, tackling me.

I think I felt a rib bruise under the pressure of her hug, but right at that moment I didn't really care. It felt good to be bruised, to feel anything at all, knowing that just a few feet away Kaylee would never feel anything again. I sniffed back a tear that I hadn't known I wanted to shed until I'd spied Mom.

"Are you okay?" she asked when she finally pulled away, her eyes scanning my face for bumps or bruises.

I nodded, not trusting myself to speak without turning into a bawling mess.

"I got here as soon as the police called me," she said, glancing at Raley.

I could see warring emotions on Raley's face. On the one hand, his headache would lessen the moment he handed me off to someone else. On the other, it was a lot easier to question a minor without her adult guardian present.

I gave Mom a quick, much-edited version of the evening's events, leaving out all the good stuff. I prayed Raley, who was listening the entire time, wouldn't feel compelled to fill them in.

When I was finished, Mom hugged me again. "You witnessed another murder!"

"Whm, nhm ehmphhm."

"What did you say?" Mom took a step back.

I sucked in a breath of air. "Well, not exactly," I repeated. "I didn't actually see her murdered."

But particulars seemed lost on her as she turned to Raley and said, "That's it. We want protection."

"No, we don't!" I protested.

"Ma'am, we don't believe your daughter is in any immediate danger."

"How can you say that?" Mom countered. "This is the second girl that's been killed."

"I assure you that we are doing everything we can to keep the student body safe."

"Maybe a trip?" Mom said, turning to me. "Would you like to go on a trip?"

"Mom, I have a trig test," I protested. Not to mention Deep Blogger was still out there somewhere, with information that might lead to the real killer, and I was the only one she was willing to spill it to.

"We could do a road trip. How fun would that be?"

Me and Mom stuck in a car together for hours on end? About as fun as shoving daggers into my eyes.

"Actually, Mrs. Featherstone," Raley cut in, "we believe the best thing to do in this situation is for her to maintain her normal routine."

Yeah, and stay where he could keep an eye on me.

It took another fifteen minutes of this back-and-forth before Raley finally convinced my mom that there wasn't a big target on my back, and I didn't need to either (A) move a hundred miles away, or (B) change my name and enter witness protection as Jane Smith from Ohio.

By the time Mom bundled me into the back of her minivan and drove home, I was beyond beat.

"Do you need to talk?" Mom asked as we pulled into our driveway. "There's still cake in the fridge."

I shook my head. As tempting as thick frosting sounded, what I needed was about a million hours of sleep.

And to figure out the identity of one Deep Blogger.

"So what happened?" Sam asked, hiking her backpack up on her shoulder.

A loaded question.

I'd been fielding texts and IMs all morning as news

had spread of Kaylee's death. And, more specifically, me discovering her. Of course, Sam, being at the center of the gossip hive, had been the first to call me, going into a chorus of *ohmigod*s and *are you all right*s and then some more *ohmigod*s. Once I'd assured her I was fine, she'd demanded all the deets. I'd promised to deliver them to her at school. When my mom wasn't listening outside my door, ready to ship me off to a deserted island at the slightest sound of trouble.

"You just, like, found her?" Sam pressed.

I nodded. "Actually I tripped over her."

"Ewwwww! You poor thing!" Sam hugged me around my backpack. "So, what happened to her?"

I looked over my left shoulder. Ashley Stanic and Cole Perkins had their heads together, whispering and glancing my way. A little farther down the hall, a couple mathletes were shooting me sympathetic looks. Mathletes! Having sympathy! For me!

"I don't know." I sighed, shutting my locker and starting for first period. "Kaylee was dead when I got there."

"Freaky," Sam said, falling into step beside me. "How'd she die?"

"I overheard the coroner say 'exsanguination.'"

Sam wrinkled up her freckled nose. "Which means ...?"

"She bled to death. Someone hit her on the back of the head, then took off."

Sam did a mock shudder. "Sick."

"No kidding." I'd tossed my Nikes directly into the washing machine when I'd gotten home, peeling them off with my mom's rubber kitchen gloves and turning the water to scalding hot. Then washed them again. And even though they'd ended up a bright, sparkling good-as-new white, I hadn't been able to force myself to put them on this morning, wearing Uggs with my jeans instead.

"What about Deep Blogger?" Sam asked. "Did he show?"

I nodded. "She. Deep Blogger's a girl."

"Did you talk to her?"

"Kinda."

"What do you mean, 'kinda'?"

"She bolted." I told Sam about my encounter and the fact I'd been seconds from learning the identity of Courtney's killer when DB had taken off.

"Do you think she saw the killer on the field?"

I shook my head. "Not likely. I would have noticed someone else out there with us. Honestly, I think she probably saw Kaylee, got scared, and ran."

"That's some coincidence, Kaylee being killed right where you were having your meeting."

I nodded. "Yeah, more than a coincidence, I'd say. Whoever killed Kaylee must have been someone who knew I would be there."

"Okay, so who knew about your midnight meeting?"

"Me. You. Chase." I thought back to the argument Chase and I had had in the hallway yesterday about my meeting. The very loud argument. "And anyone within earshot of my locker."

"Or, in the text network of anyone with earshot," Sam pointed out. "That doesn't narrow it down a whole lot, does it?"

"No. Not a whole lot." Which left us back at square one. Again.

As we rounded the corner, I spotted Chase leaning against the doorframe of my first period class. He was dressed today in a pair of low-slung jeans, and a black T-shirt with a black long sleeve underneath. A chain hung off the side of his jeans, and in place of his usual boots, he had on a well-worn pair of black Chucks, giving him a modern-day James Dean vibe. While the outfit might make anyone else look like he was trying just a little too hard at the "brooding-teen" thing, on him it looked completely authentic.

"Hey," he asked when we approached. "You okay?"

I nodded. "Mostly."

"She tripped on Kaylee's dead body," Sam supplied.

Chase nodded. "Yeah, I saw."

I blinked at him. "What do you mean you 'saw'?"

"I was there. You didn't really think I'd let you go meet some anonymous stranger in the middle of the night by yourself, did you?"

I rolled my eyes. "Seriously?" Though, I had to admit, part of me went kinda warm at the thought of him fancying himself my protector.

"Why didn't you say anything?" I asked.

"I was hiding. Deep Blogger wanted to talk to you alone, so I stayed back near the snack hut. I figured I could keep an eye on you from there and jump in if anything shady went down."

"I'd call a dead body pretty shady," Sam pointed out.

"Right. As soon as I heard you scream, I ran after you, but that detective got to you first. You're wicked fast," he observed.

"Yeah. Dead bodies bring out the track star in me."

"Anyway, as soon as I saw the detective, I left. I figured you were safe, and, well, let's just say I don't have the best relationship with the police."

Gee, I wonder why.

"Did you see Deep Blogger?" I asked.

He nodded. "Took off toward the back parking lot. I tried to follow him as soon as I saw you were okay, but he was long gone by then."

"She," Sam said. "Deep Blogger's a girl."

"Who?" Chase asked me.

Reluctantly, I shook my head. "I couldn't tell. It was dark, and she was wearing all black. But she had a female voice."

"You're sure?"

I nodded. "Pretty sure. She was trying to disguise it, but it was high. I guess it *could* have been a guy, but I doubt it."

He frowned, his forehead wrinkling into a thoughtful pose. "And she didn't tell you what she saw?"

"Just that she saw someone go into Josh's house that day. She was about to tell me who it was when she took off."

"Did she see them come out?"

I shrugged. "I didn't get a chance to ask."

The bell rang, and Sam shoved her backpack up onto her shoulder. "Duty calls. I'll catch you after statistics, cool?" she called over her shoulder.

"I'll text you," I promised.

"Okay, let's go," Chase said to me, pushing off the wall.

"Go where?" I narrowed my eyes at him.

"We need to track down this Blogger chick."

"But I have lit now," I protested.

He shot me a look that clearly said James Dean thought I was a geek. "Ditch it."

"I can't do that."

"Why not?"

I bit my lip. Because I'd already done it twice in the last week. Once more and it would mean a note home, just one more thing for my mom to freak about. I'd caught her looking at boarding school brochures online this morning. I had a feeling I was two seconds away from parental lockdown as it was, never mind what would happen if she found out I was cutting class, too.

On the other hand . . .

It hadn't escaped my notice that the sea of people rushing to class had created a wide berth around yours truly. While most people were bumping into one another, I could reach both hands out to either side and not touch a single soul. It was as if death was catching and I was ground zero for the virus. I had a bad feeling that my social life as I knew it was officially over. Unless I wanted to forever be "that girl," I needed to find the real killer and fast.

"Fine," I finally gave in. "What's one more day of juvenile delinquency?"

FOURTEEN

"SO, WHERE ARE WE GOING?" I ASKED AS I FOLLOWED Chase down the now empty hall. I fought the urge to duck at each classroom window we passed.

"Library," he said. "We need a computer."

He led the way out of the main building and to the right. It wasn't until he made another right into the side parking lot that I realized we weren't going on foot.

"Oh, no. No way." I stopped in my tracks.

Chase spun around. "What?"

"No way am I getting in a car with you again."

He cocked his head, the beginnings of amusement playing at the corner of his lips. "And why not?"

"Because you drive like a maniac."

"I do not."

"How many speeding tickets have you gotten?"

"This month?"

"I rest my case."

"I'm joking," he said, the grin taking full bloom. "Come on, I'll drive slow for you, *Granny*."

I shook my head. "I've seen enough dead bodies for one lifetime, thanks. I think I'll walk."

He shrugged. "Okay, suit yourself." Then he called over his shoulder, "Meet you there!" before continuing on to his Camaro, tucked in the second row between two used SUVs.

I took the sidewalk the two blocks, perfectly content with my decision even when Chase roared past me at decidedly *not* Granny speeds a couple minutes later. The weather was nice, the street deserted, and the physical exercise was a welcome distraction from the mental workout I'd been doing ever since finding Kaylee. Had the same person killed both Courtney and Kaylee? Why? Had Kaylee known something about the killer's identity? What had she been doing on the football field? And how did Deep Blogger fit into all this? I didn't know. And, sadly, by the time I reached the library, I was no closer to figuring it out.

I made my way down to the basement, where the one-hour computers were located. Chase was already typing away at one near the end of the row, and I pulled up a plastic chair and sat down beside him.

"So, what's your plan for tracking down our Deep Blogger?" I asked.

"We're going to trace her IP address," he said, not looking up from the screen. "I should have done this yesterday when the email first came in," he chided himself, "but I was kind of preoccupied with finding out what she had to say."

"Well, let's hope she's still feeling chatty. How do we find the IP address?" I asked.

"Here's the original email she sent," he said, pointing to the screen. "We need to trace where it came from to get to the *Homepage*'s in-box." He clicked a couple buttons on the side of the open email in-box window, and another window popped up, creating an email header three times the normal size, filled with tons of numbers and periods in seemingly random patterns.

"What is that?" I asked, squinting at the screen.

"It's a list of the IP addresses of all the servers the email traveled through." He stabbed his finger at a line farthest down. "See that one? That's where it originated. That's Deep Blogger's computer."

"Cool!" I paused. "Okay, so what do we do with the IP address? It doesn't tell us where she is, does it?"

"Not yet," he answered. Then he pulled up another window. "How we doing on time?" he asked.

I looked down at my cell screen. "We've been on twenty minutes."

"Perfect. Okay, now we look up where the IP is on a

search site." He pulled a page called ARIN Whois and typed the line of letters into the search box. A couple seconds later the registration info for that address popped up on the screen.

Chase stared at it. "That can't be right."

"Why? What does it say?" I asked, looking over his shoulder.

The name on the screen was a Jackson Building Supply. There was an address in downtown San José listed beside it.

"So some builder is Deep Blogger?" I asked. He was right. That didn't make much sense.

But Chase shook his head. "The IP address is owned by this company, but I think I know who sent the actual email."

"Who?"

"Shiloh Jackson. Her dad owns Jackson Building Supply."

Now *that* made sense.

Shiloh and I had both been in a school production of *The Jungle Book* when we were in fifth grade—me as an ape and her as a snake—but since hitting middle school, we'd gone in completely different social directions. Shiloh was a Goth girl all the way, looking more vampiric than human these days. Black on black with black on top of that. Kind of like Chase to the nth degree. The only thing about her that wasn't midnight black was her pale skin, powdered to look almost deathly white.

As you can imagine, Shiloh and her cohorts were the polar opposites of the Color Guard girls. The Goths thought the Color Guard girls were Barbie clones. The Color Guard girls thought the Goths were vampire freaks. Even so, the two factions kept to their separate corners of HHH. Which made me wonder why Shiloh had been anywhere in the vicinity of the chastity queen on the day she died.

"So, let's go talk to Shiloh," I said.

But Chase was still shaking his head, staring at the screen. "You know what, I'm gonna let you take this one solo."

I froze, raising an eyebrow his way. "And why is that?"

He shrugged. "I just think you can handle this one on your own. Go, young grasshopper, show me what you've got."

Hmm. Chase saying he didn't want to be present when we interviewed the person who could potentially break this case wide open was like Andi Brackenridge saying she didn't believe in eyeliner. Something was up.

But, if it meant not having him look over my shoulder, I wasn't going to protest talking to Shiloh alone.

"Suit yourself," I said. I slipped my book bag on my shoulder. "I'll call you later and let you know what I find out."

"Yeah. You do that," he said, his voice distracted, his eyes still on the screen.

I tried to shrug off the feeling that I was missing something as I headed back to school.

It was lunch period before I had a chance to track Shiloh down. She and her posse hung out at the 7-Eleven across the street from the high school, smoking unfiltered cigarettes in a show of defiant rebellion. The school had a strict no smoking policy—it was against the rules to light a cigarette anywhere within twenty feet of school grounds. The Goths sat twenty feet and two inches away, puffing like chimneys. Take that, establishment!

I hiked my bag a little higher on my shoulders and made my way toward their little group. I got within four feet before all eyes turned my way.

Two guys in black leather jackets sat next to Shiloh and another girl that I didn't recognize. Though, I'll admit, I hardly recognized Shiloh. In fifth grade she'd been on the chubby side, with big fat chipmunk cheeks and dimples. Her light brown hair had been forever in a ponytail, and she'd had a thing for Pokemon-themed T-shirts.

Her T-shirt today had a horse's head dismembered from its bloody body, advertising some band I'd (thankfully) never heard of. Her hair was harsh black with one big, blue streak painted across the front. Sort of like a smurfy skunk. She wore a black miniskirt over a pair of black-and-white striped stockings and Doc Martens on her feet. A black sweater held together with big silver safety pins capped off the outfit.

And while a thin film of baby fat still clung to her cheeks, the rest of her was rail thin. Like, super rail. I had a feeling the cigarette in her right hand qualified as lunch.

"Um, hi," I said, walking up to her.

She gave me a blank stare back.

I cleared my throat, hoping the gesture didn't seem as nervous as I felt. While I knew that behind the scary makeup and horse-head T-shirts the Goths were just regular sixteen-year-olds like me, the vampire-inspired personas they were rocking were just a tad intimidating.

"Uh, it's Hartley. From Mrs. Edgemon's class? Fifth grade?"

She blinked at me. "I know."

"Oh."

"You're that chick that keeps finding dead people."

Mental face palm.

"Um, sorta."

"I heard you found Kaylee's body last night," the guy to her right piped up. His skin was painted white, his eyes rimmed in black like a character from *The Nightmare Before Christmas*.

I nodded reluctantly. "Yeah."

"What was it like?"

"Finding her? Scary, I guess."

He shook his head. "No, the dead body. Was she, like, gutted or something?"

I shook my head.

"Oh."

I was more than a little creeped out by how disappointed he sounded.

"Um, anyway, I need to talk to you, Shiloh," I said.

Again she gave me the blank stare. " 'Kay. Talk."

"Uh, maybe we could go somewhere more private?"

"Why?"

"I have a few questions. About *blogging*," I said, adding a little hint-hint, nudge-nudge to my voice. "*Deep blogging*."

I felt myself gain a distinct upper hand as she went a shade paler.

With a quick glance at her friends, she did a deceptively casual shrug. "Fine. Let's walk."

I could feel the eyes of her companions on my back as we moved a few paces away. Shiloh led the way to the side of the building, waiting until we moved behind a big green Dumpster before lighting up another cigarette. Her hand shook as she took the first drag.

"What do you want to know?" she asked, exhaling smoke through her nose.

"You are Deep Blogger, aren't you?"

Shiloh glanced over one shoulder. Then the other. Reassured that only the stale donuts and breakfast-burrito remains in the Dumpster could hear us, she nodded. "Yeah."

Score one for Chase.

"How did you find out?" she asked.

"We traced your IP address."

"Sucks. I didn't think of that." She took another drag.

"Why did you run last night?" I asked.

"Are you serious?" she asked, her heavily lined eyes going wide. "I stumbled on a freakin' dead body. Did you see the blood?"

I nodded, ignoring the way my stomach suddenly seized up as I remembered my tainted Nikes.

"Anyway, when I saw that, I just panicked. I ran, you know? I mean what if the killer was still there?"

"Was he?" I asked. "Did you see him?"

She shook her head. "The only person I saw was you."

Which brought me to the point of this interrogation. "You were about to tell me who killed Courtney when you ran."

She did another over-the-shoulder look. She took a deep breath, then a deep drag from her cigarette. (Which totally negated the deep breath, if you asked me.)

"God, where do I start?" she said.

"Anywhere you want as long as you don't run away again before you get to the good part."

She nodded. "I have a blog. It's called The Mainstream Sucks."

Not the most original name, but I nodded, motioning for her to go on.

"Anyway, last year the Color Guard girls tried to get me to sign an abstinence pledge. I told them it was a little late to put the virgin back in the barn, ya know?"

No, I didn't, being still in the barn myself. But I nodded again anyway.

"Well, when I told Courtney and her clones where they could shove their pledge, they TPed my house."

"That sucks," I commented.

"Big-time. My dad had to hire a tree service to come remove the TP from the top branches of the tree out front. Cost him a thousand bucks. Which meant that instead of getting a car this year, I'm stuck riding my brother's old ten-speed. Bitch."

I was pretty sure she was referring to Courtney and not the bike.

"So, the blog?" I prompted.

"Right. Yeah, so I followed Courtney after school that next day, meaning to kick the crap out of her perky little butt. But instead I saw her at a donut shop. Stuffing her face with bear claws. Of course she went into the bathroom and ralphed it all up afterward, but the video I took on my phone of her gorging was priceless. I decided there was better payback in the world than a butt kicking. So, I went home and posted it to my blog instead. Guess how many hits I got?"

I shrugged. "How many?"

"Eight hundred. That's like half the school!"

"Dude." I was impressed.

"No kidding. Anyway, that's when I started following Courtney and her Color Guard clones on a regular basis. I got some priceless stuff, let me tell you."

I couldn't help asking. "Like what?"

"Here, lemme show you," she said, pulling out her phone. A few clicks later she connected and logged into her blogger page. A black background and bloodred words gave it a TMZ-like feel. Only instead of celebs sporting cellulite she featured Color Guard girls with their skirts accidentally tucked into their panties, fingers up their noses when they thought no one was looking, and chowing on cheeseburgers.

I scrolled down to today's featured article. It was titled "The pick of the day," beneath a picture of Caitlyn Calvin digging a wedgie out of her butt.

I couldn't help a snort of laughter. "Nice," I said, truly meaning it.

"Thanks." She grinned, showing off those dimples I remembered.

"So, I take it you were following Courtney on the day she died?"

She nodded. "Yeah. After school I heard her telling one of her clones that she got a text from Josh and needed a ride to his house. I thought maybe I'd get some good footage because, well, everyone knew she was boning Josh."

Everyone except me.

"What happened?"

"By the time I got there on my bike, I knew she'd already be inside. So I pulled around to the back of Josh's place to get a good view of his bedroom window."

"What did you see?"

"It was hard to make much out. All I could see of the room was a sliver between the curtains. But I could tell that someone else was in the room with her."

"This someone else—did you see his face?" I asked, leaning forward.

She shook her head. "No. But I know who it was."

"How?"

"I recognized his clothes. There was no mistaking him."

"And?" I asked, the suspense killing me. "Who was it?"

Shiloh bit her lip. "Look, you can't tell anyone that I

told you this. I mean it. If this guy knows I saw him, that's a target on my head. I don't want to be stuck in some witness protection thing."

I crossed my heart with my index finger. "I swear. Totally confidential."

She looked over both shoulders again. "The guy I saw?" She leaned in close. "It was Chase Erikson."

FIFTEEN

SUDDENLY EVERY CONVERSATION CHASE AND I HAD had over the last few days played through my head, taking on new meaning. Sinister meaning, I realized, as those warring puzzle pieces fell into place. Everything fit perfectly. Chase had been outside Josh's house the day of the murder. It would have been the easiest thing in the world for him to slip in, off Courtney, then slip back outside, creating a perfect alibi for himself with his photos. And he had been vehemently against me meeting Deep Blogger the first time. Had it been out of concern for my safety, as he claimed, or because he was worried that someone really had seen him go into Josh's house? And what about Kaylee? He'd admitted to being at the football field. Had it been to protect me or to kill Kaylee?

Everywhere a dead body had been lately, so had Chase.

I felt sick.

And the fact that Shiloh was blowing another nervous mouthful of smoke in my face didn't help.

"Are you sure?" I asked, really, *really* hoping she wasn't. "You're sure it was Chase?"

Shiloh nodded so vigorously her black bangs bounced against her forehead. "Positive."

"But you said you didn't see his face."

"He had his back turned to me," she conceded.

"Then how can you be sure it was Chase? I mean, lots of guys could look like him from the back." Which wasn't entirely true—Chase had a style all his own. Not to mention that there were precious few guys at our school who were over six feet, broad shouldered, built like gym rats, but dressed like James Dean. "Did you see his hair?" I asked, grasping. "Check his height, see a telltale mole or something?"

Shiloh shook her head. "Give me a break—it was just a glimpse through the curtains."

"Then how can you be sure it was him?"

"I recognized the hoodie he was wearing. It had an eagle on the back. A big purple one."

I felt my stomach twist painfully. She was right. I'd seen Chase wear that very same hoodie.

"That's Chase's hoodie all right," I conceded.

"I know. I gave it to him."

I cocked my head. "*You* gave it to him?"

"For his birthday last year. We were dating."

I did a cartoon-worthy double take. "Chase was dating *you*?!" I said. Then immediately felt guilty as her expression hardened. "Sorry, I didn't mean that the way it sounded. I'm sure lots of guys want to date you. You're very . . . uh . . . unique."

Which, as I assessed her anew, was actually very true. Not only unique, but she also had a flair of the exotic about her. Something forbidden. And . . . if you stripped away all the affected makeup and funky clothes, Shiloh was actually kinda pretty. I gave her an up and down. Okay, *very* pretty. She was thin with long legs that looked great in a miniskirt (even if the miniskirt was covered in zippers and safety pins and the legs were encased in Wicked Witch of the West tights). And, unlike most model-thin girls, she actually had a chest. One which was shown off to advantage in the tight horse-head T-shirt.

She was a bad girl, Chase was a bad boy; they fit perfectly. I shouldn't have been surprised to find that their romantic paths had crossed at some point.

And it shouldn't have mattered to me at all. And it didn't. That little dip in my stomach had nothing to do with the fact that *this* was the kind of girl that was really Chase's type. It was probably because I'd skipped breakfast. That's it, I was just hungry.

" . . . and then I—Hey, are you even listening?"

"Yes." No. I realized that I'd totally spaced out on what she'd been saying.

"Uh-huh. Well, anyway, I was saying that I was working on the *Homepage* last year, and he was the editor, and you know how those late-night sessions go, right?"

"Right." No, I didn't. And for some reason that dip deepened at the thought. "Okay, let's assume it was Chase you saw. Why would he want to kill Courtney?"

"How should I know? Maybe it was an accident. Maybe she caught him breaking into Josh's house. Weren't Josh's parents away?"

"Yeah, so?"

"Perfect time to break in and grab some stuff."

I shook my head. I had a hard time believing there was anything in Josh's room that would appeal to Chase. On the other hand . . . what did I really know about Bad Boy except that, well, he was a bad boy? But just how bad was he?

"I don't know," I hedged. "That doesn't really sound like Chase."

Shiloh narrowed her eyes at me. "Yeah, well, I'll bet I know him a whole lot better than you do."

I bit my lip. "That may be true, but—"

"Chase is a jerk," Shiloh jumped in before I could finish. "A two-faced, coldhearted, reptilian creep."

I raised an eyebrow. "I take it things didn't end on a

friendly note between you?"

"He dumped me via Twitter."

"Ouch."

"No kidding. One day everything's great, the next I'm being tweet dumped for no reason. No explanation. Nothing. What a jerk," she said, taking another long drag.

I'll admit, it was a pretty callous way of ending a relationship. On the other hand, Shiloh seemed just pissed enough about it to want a little revenge. And accusing someone of murder is a heck of a way to get back at him.

"You sure your personal feelings aren't clouding your judgment a little here?"

Shiloh shot me a look, then shrugged. "I'll admit, he's not my favorite person. But I know what I saw. Which is why you cannot tell anyone it was me that told you this. If Chase knew that it was me who saw him with Courtney, can you imagine how pissed he'd be?"

Uh-oh.

"Um, about that . . ." I trailed off.

Shiloh narrowed her eyes at me. "What?"

"Chase was kinda the one who traced your IP address."

"What?! Christ, what part of 'come alone' don't you understand?"

"Sorry! How was I supposed to know he was the one you didn't want to know? I mean, you had to know he was going to read the tip you sent in to the paper."

"Yeah, which is why I sent it *anonymously*. Geez." Shiloh crushed her cigarette butt under the toe of her Docs and immediately dug into the side pocket of her sweater to pull out another one. Her hands shook as she lit it. "Great! This is just great," she said, the cancer stick bobbing up and down between her lips as she began to pace. "What am I going to do now? He knows I saw!"

"Look, he doesn't know anything except that you're Deep Blogger. I'll just tell him that you didn't really get a good look at the guy."

She spun on me, eyes narrowed. "You better, Hartley Featherstone, or I'm gonna hunt you down and beat you senseless."

Scary thing? I totally believed her.

"Right. Cool. No problem. Hey, you can totally count on me. Okay, well, I'm gonna just go now," I said, slowly backing away.

"I know where you live, Hartley!" she yelled after me. "This is all your fault!"

Why did everyone think that stumbling on dead bodies was somehow my fault? Like I wanted to stumble on them. Like this was my idea of a good time. Trust me, between wearing braces for the entirety of my high school experience and finding one more dead body, I'd totally take the metal mouth torture.

Only, as long as the killer was still out there, the fates

seemed intent on making my life suck like a black hole.

As soon as I got back on campus, I texted Sam.

where r u?

Thirty seconds later a response buzzed my phone to life.

cftria. y?

need 2 tlk. brt.

Five minutes later, I hit the cafeteria. It was packed with hungry students, the melded noise of dozens of conversations bouncing off the poorly insulated walls, the smell of spaghetti, mystery meatballs, and extrastrength disinfectant permeating the air.

I spied Sam sitting at a table near the middle of the room with Kyle and Erin Carter and Jessica Hanson, both still wearing their mourning armbands. I made a beeline for them, grabbing my best friend by the arm as soon as I could reach her.

"Hey, we need to talk. Pronto."

"Whoa, chill," she said, as I jostled her box of organic grape juice, spilling purple stuff on the table.

"I'm serious. This is, like, life and death."

Poor word choice. Jessica raised an eyebrow at me, then sent a look to Erin.

"Uh, we were just leaving anyway," Jessica said, gathering her tray of pizza sticks and spaghetti. She elbowed Erin, who did the same, moving to a spot a few tables away next to some guys from the track team. And, I noticed, skirting the long way around the table to avoid getting too close to me in the process.

I rolled my eyes.

But I had bigger fish to fry. Sam and I had possibly been in cahoots with a killer.

"We're possibly in cahoots with a killer," I said to Sam as soon as Jessica and Erin were out of earshot.

Kyle wrinkled his forehead up. "What's a cahoots?"

"Hart, what are you talking about?" Sam asked, wiping at the juice spill with a paper napkin.

I quickly filled them in on my meeting with Shiloh and her revelation that the killer had been wearing Chase's eagle hoodie.

"Did she say for sure that it was Chase in the hoodie?" Kyle asked when I was done.

"No," I hedged. "She said she never saw the guy's face."

"So, isn't it possible it was someone else?" Sam asked.

I shrugged. "Possible, I guess, but hecka coincidental, isn't it? I mean, he just happens to be there at the time of the murder, and the killer just happens to be wearing his clothes? Then Chase just happens to offer to help us catch the killer, instead completely throwing us off the real trail."

"Has he?" Kyle asked.

"Has he what?"

"Thrown you off the trail? I mean, it kinda sounds like he's been helping you."

"Right. Which is exactly what he'd *want* us to think if he was the killer."

"She has a point," Sam said. "So what do we do now?"

"I don't know. But, I tell you what we don't do."

"What's that?"

"Tell Chase what Shiloh saw."

As if on cue, the doors to the cafeteria opened and I spied our newest suspect pushing through.

He walked up to the lunch counter, grabbed a tray, and threw a slice of lukewarm pizza and a Coke on it.

Not exactly nefarious, but I guess even killers had to eat lunch.

"Let's go confront him," Kyle said, standing up.

I grabbed his arm. "Are you kidding? Sit down."

His butt thumped back onto the chair with a thud.

"What if we're wrong?" I asked. "What if Shiloh was mistaken? Or lying!" Though, even as I said it, I had to count that theory as a long shot. Even if Shiloh did hold some wounded ex-girlfriend grudge against Chase, the look in her eyes when she'd talked about seeing the killer had been pure fear. No doubt about it, she'd been afraid of Chase.

Still, it was possible she'd been mistaken. . . .

Sam shrugged. "Okay, so what if he's innocent? We

confront him, he denies it, we're good to go."

"Wrong. If he's innocent, we've just totally pissed him off and there goes his help catching the killer."

"But what if we're right?" she countered.

"If we're right, we've just accused him of being a killer. That kinda puts us on his short list of future killees."

Sam scrunched up her nose. "Good point. It's a lose-lose."

"Come on, let's get out of here," I said, grabbing her by the sleeve again and tugging her toward the back door.

"Dude. This is a fifty-dollar shirt. You stretch it out, you buy a new one."

I let go of her sleeve. "Sorry." But I ducked my head, the three of us scuttling toward the back of the cafeteria. We hit the door just as Chase paid for his food and turned around to scan the room for a seat. For half a second I could swear his eyes were searching for *me*, but I shook it off, quickly pushing outside.

No sooner had we stepped outside into the sunshine than my cell chirped to life. I looked down at the readout. A text from Chase:

where r u?

I bit my lip. So he had been looking for me.

busy. why?

did u talk to Shiloh?

Despite the fact that I wasn't 110 percent sure I believed

Shiloh had actually seen Chase in Josh's house, I had promised to keep Shiloh's observations confidential. Besides, it was better to be safe than sorry.

ya. no help. she didn't c bg.

A second later he texted back:

bg?

bad guy, I clarified.

A few seconds later my cell chirped again.

cute.

I really wished he'd stop calling me that. Especially if he was a killer.

so shiloh was no help?

no. not a reliable witness.

At least, it was safer for her if he thought that. Me? I had a sinking feeling she was a very reliable witness.

bummer.

I was just about to text back, when Chris Fret came running through the quad, heading toward the front of the main building.

"Dude," he called when he spotted us. "Did you guys hear?"

"Hear what?" Kyle asked.

"There's a news van parked out front again," he said. He started dancing backward. "Word is, they're interviewing students for the news tonight."

"Not again," I mumbled.

"We're gonna go see if we can be those jerks in the background waving to Mom." Chris grinned, looking like it was his life's dream to be a jerk.

We followed him around to the front of the quad, pausing as we hit the lawn. Sure enough, a KTVU news van was parked outside again, a satellite on its roof, cables leading across the lawn to the camera guy. Next to him stood the intern, and a couple of feet away was Diane Dancy. She held a microphone in one hand and fluffed her hair with the other. Beside her, Caitlyn was checking her lip gloss in a compact and carefully posing so the sunlight hit her highlights at just the right angle.

A small group of people had gathered behind them, other aspiring jerks sticking their tongues out at the camera and yelling things like "Go, Wildcats!"

"Check one, two, three," the intern said into Diane's microphone.

The guy under the camera gave him a thumbs-up, and the intern nodded at Diane.

She shook her hair out one more time, then looked straight in the camera as the intern counted her down. "We're on in five, four, three, two . . ." Then he trailed off, pointing at the reporter.

"This is Diane Dancy reporting live in front of Herbert Hoover High School in San José where a second innocent student has been found brutally murdered this week. The body of young, vivacious Kaylee Clark was discovered last night on the deserted football field, viciously bludgeoned to death."

I shivered as I remembered the scene. Despite the warm sunshine hitting me, goose bumps broke out on my arms.

"Like the first victim," the reporter went on, "Kaylee was a member of the very popular Color Guard on campus."

The use of the adverb "very" was a bit of a stretch, but it was clear Diane was a woman who used modifiers to squeeze every last drop of drama from a situation.

Though, to be honest, this one was an easy squeeze.

"I have beside me one of their fellow students, Caitlyn Calvin. Caitlyn, how has this tragedy affected you?"

Caitlyn sniffed, her face showing what I would swear was genuine emotion.

"Kaylee and Courtney were my best friends in the whole world," she told the camera. "I don't know what I'm going to do without them." She did a little sob, a single tear rolling down her face. Though I noticed it wasn't actually enough to mess up her mascara in front of the camera. Cool trick. I wondered if she'd practiced it in front of the mirror or if it was a natural talent of Color Guard girls.

"What can you tell us about the other Color Guard members' reaction to Kaylee's brutal death?"

"We're scared, Diane," Caitlyn said. "It's clear that a

serial killer is targeting members of the Color Guard."

While two people hardly qualified as serial, I had to admit that Caitlyn might have a point. It had to be more than coincidence that both Kaylee and Courtney had been killed. Was someone targeting them because of their abstinence beliefs? Was this less a personal vendetta than a moral one?

And, if it was, did that mean the killer wasn't done? With both Courtney and Kaylee gone, there was one obvious target left.

And apparently she knew it, as she looked straight into the camera, her eyes shining with tears.

"I implore the police to find the persons responsible for these murders," Caitlyn choked out. "Because if they don't"—short pause for another sob—"I fear I may be next!"

SIXTEEN

I HAD TO ADMIT THAT IN CAITLYN'S POSITION, I'D BE A little scared, too. As the lone purple clone left, it was entirely possible that Caitlyn was a sitting duck.

Which is why, as the bell rang, I decided that I had to talk to her. If someone did have a Color Guard grudge, she was the one person who might be able to shed some light on it. Unfortunately, Caitlyn spent fifth period in the grief counselor's office. Then she had sixth period lit in the west wing while I had trig in the east, meaning that by the time the final bell rang and I was free to stalk my prey, she'd already left campus in her cute little Volkswagen Rabbit. (At least that's what Ashley Stannic said when I caught up to her in the parking lot.) Luckily, according to Chris Fret, Caitlyn worked at Hollister in the Oakridge Mall after school on Wednesdays, Thursdays, and Fridays. The mall was a ten-minute ride down Blossom Hill Road if you had a car. Or a half-hour bus ride with the homeless and mentally challenged if you didn't.

Needless to say, fifteen minutes later, Sam and I were pleading our case to Kevin.

"Look, we just need to borrow the car for a few minutes. An hour, tops."

He lifted his head from the sofa where he was lying, totally engrossed in a rerun of *Meerkat Manor*.

"I dunno," he hedged, licking brownie dough off a plastic spatula. A bowl of mix sat in front of him, an empty box and bottle of water beside it on the coffee table. Apparently the munchies had hit before Kev could bake his brownies.

"We won't go far," I promised. "The mall is practically down the street."

"The mall?" He looked up, a small glob of fudgey stuff clinging to the side of his mouth. "That's the epitome of our capitalist materialistic society. I can't even begin to tell you the horrors of the environmental and humanitarian crimes that are committed in the name of the almighty dollar at the mall."

Seriously? It was a Cheesecake Factory and a couple of department stores. It wasn't like they were killing puppies.

"We won't buy anything," I promised. "We just need to talk to someone there."

"Who?" he asked, shoving another spatulaful into his mouth.

"Caitlyn Calvin. She works at Hollister."

"Hollister? Dude, they, like, employ monkeys to sew their clothes!"

Sam put her hands on her hips. "Monkeys? Really?"

Kevin wrinkled his forehead. "Or maybe kids. Some workers that are really not cool."

I vaguely wondered if those brownies were the "funny" variety.

"Look, we just need to talk to her," I said, "about the deaths at the school. Both girls were her friends."

"Dude. I heard about that. You found them. Both." He gave me a long look.

"I had nothing to do with it!" I protested.

He narrowed his eyes at me. "You sure?"

"That I didn't kill two people? Yeah, kinda."

Luckily, his brain was too full of holes to detect my sarcasm. "Okay. If you say so, I trust you, dude."

"So . . . the car?" Sam asked. "Can we please borrow it?"

Kevin nodded, spooning more brownie goo into his mouth. "Yeah, sure. Knock yourself out. But she needs fuel."

Uh-oh.

"You mean veggie oil?" I asked.

He nodded.

I hated to even ask. . . . "Okay. So, where do we get five gallons of veggie oil?"

"I suggest Burger Barn."

Oh boy. The bus was looking better and better.

After helping Kevin find his keys ("Dude, like they were just here a second ago . . . oh, there they are. Under the brownie mix. Dude, want some brownie mix? It's killer."), Sam and I said a silent prayer to the gods of canola that we had enough fuel to drive the three blocks to Burger Barn.

Luckily, we had just enough, the Volvo giving a surrender cough as we glided into the parking lot and slid into a slot. Inside, three guys manned the registers—a twenty-something with pimples, an Indian guy with a mustache that looked like it needed its own hairnet, and a guy I recognized from my fourth period Spanish class.

"Hey," I said, catching his attention.

He looked up from his register and squinted his eyes as if he were in denial about needing glasses. A second later recognition dawned on him. "Senorita Gonzalez's class?"

I nodded. "Hartley."

"Right. You're the one that keeps finding dead chicks."

Of all the things I aspired to be known for . . .

"Anyway," Sam jumped in, knowing this was a touchy

subject, "we were wondering if we could have some of your grease?"

He raised an eyebrow, his eyes darting to the visibly greasy countertop.

"For our car," she explained. "It's an SVO-converted engine, and we're out of veggie oil."

"Oh." He thought for a moment. "Sure, I guess. I mean, we usually just throw that stuff out."

Score.

"How much do you want?"

"How much do you have?"

"We've got a couple drums outside. Meet me around back," he instructed.

We did, circling the building to the service entrance where Spanish Class Guy emerged from a minute later.

He pointed to a huge drum sitting near the Dumpster. "She's all yours."

The drum was almost as tall as I was; twice as wide; and had white, pus-looking stuff oozing out the top. Like a giant zit.

Lucky us.

"You got a funnel or something?" Spanish Class Guy asked.

Sam shook her head.

"Hmmm." He stroked his chin where the first wisps of a goatee were trying their darnedest to grow. "Well, we've got some plastic gloves in the back. I guess you could just use your hands."

I tried really hard to suppress a gag.

Two minutes later, Spanish Class Guy returned with a pair of plastic food-prep gloves. He gave one to each of us, then tossed a "Good luck" over his shoulder before disappearing back into Burger Barn.

Sam and I looked at each other.

"I guess we should dig in," she said.

I nodded. "Yep."

Neither of us moved.

"Okay. Let's go."

"Okay," I agreed.

"You gonna move soon?"

"Me? Why should I go first?"

"It's *your* boyfriend that got us into this."

"*Ex*-boyfriend. Besides, it's your brother's stupid eco car."

We both looked at the Volvo. Then the drum. Then the teeny plastic gloves again.

"Fine!" I threw my hands up, giving in. "I'll go first."

I slipped the gloves on, then closed my eyes and shoved one hand into the vat of grease.

Oh. My. God.

It was soft and squishy, and it smelled like rancid meat. I clamped my mouth shut to keep my lunch down as I

shoved one handful of gooey grossness into the fuel converter. That's it, I was never eating anything cooked in oil
ever again.

"Is it totally sick?" Sam asked, scrunching up her nose
as she watched me.

"Nope," I lied. "I'm good. Dig in."

She looked a little green, but she did, shoving one
gloved hand into the vat.

"Oh. My. God. This is so gross!"

"Breathe through your mouth. It doesn't smell as bad
that way."

She nodded, the two of us panting as we shoved handful after handful into the converter.

Twenty minutes later we had shoved enough goo down
the converter to get us to Oakridge and back. We hopped
into the car, a stream of cheeseburger-scented smoke trailing in our wake. I prayed no one we knew saw us. Or
smelled us.

Saving the environment was so gross.

The Oakridge Mall is home to every possible store you
could ever want to shop at. Target, Macy's, Old Navy,
Sears, as well as all the usual mall staples, including Hot
Topic, the Gap, and Hollister. It also houses a food court,
a full movie theater, a P.F. Chang's, a Cheesecake Factory,
and a California Pizza Kitchen. I could happily live my
entire life at this mall.

The only downside was that as they built more stores over the years, they ran out of room to build out the parking lot. We circled for fifteen full minutes before spotting a lady with a loaded stroller and two kids exiting Target. We car stalked her to the back of the parking garage (eliciting odd looks as we filled the entire lower section of the parking structure with burger smoke) and waited while she loaded the bigger kid into the back, the baby into the car seat, and the stroller into the trunk of her beige SUV. A truck came down the other aisle, peering at our prized spot, but Sam pointed to her blinker, honked aggressively at him, and he moved on. (I'm sure it was the honk that did it, not the fact that our smoke was starting to cloud the air.)

Once we seized parking victory, we cruised down the main thoroughfare of the crowded mall and made our way to the Hollister store, situated between the Victoria's Secret and Borders. We paused to enjoy the larger-than-life man-candy image on the front wall of a guy wearing nothing but low-slung Hollister jeans before pressing inside to find Caitlyn.

We spied her right away at a display near the back, folding piles of pink T-shirts with sparkly peace-sign designs on them. (Cute. I wondered if they were on sale. . . .)

The second Caitlyn's eyes lifted from the crop-sleeved T in her hand to meet mine, she let out a little scream. "You! Stay away from me! You're the angel of death!" She jumped back, putting one hand out in front of her as if to ward off evil spirits.

Oh, brother.

"Relax, Caitlyn. I'm not armed."

"That's not funny. Because of you, two of my best friends are dead."

"I didn't kill them!"

But Caitlyn nodded vigorously, still keeping a good three feet between us. "Every time you go near someone, they die. You're cursed!"

This time I did a real eye roll. "Seriously?"

"I'm not dead," Sam pointed out. "And I hang out with Hartley all the time."

Caitlyn bit her lip, digesting the logic of this statement. "You must be immune or something."

I thought about pointing out that Caitlyn spent a lot more time with the dead girls—and therefore was way more likely an angel of death than I was—but I figured there was no sense in pissing off my prime witness. Instead, I tried to ease her mind with flattery.

"Nice shirt," I said, pointing to the sparkly purple thing she had on. Honestly, it looked exactly like the one she'd worn last time I'd seen her. I wondered if she bought them in bulk.

But she was vain enough to bite. "Thanks. We're sold out of these, but we have some in a more"—she paused, giving me an up-and-down look—"generous style near the register."

I'm pretty proud of myself that I managed to keep a smile on my face. "Great. Thanks. I'll check those out." Okay, it was more of a grimace. "We actually wanted to ask you a few questions. About the interview you did this morning."

At the mention of her KTVU debut, Caitlyn softened a little. "You saw that?"

I nodded.

"How did I look on camera?"

Her grief was touching.

"You looked fabulous."

She tossed her hair over her right shoulder. "They said they might do a follow-up next week."

"You said that someone was targeting members of the Color Guard," I reminded her. "What did you mean by that?"

"Well, I think it's pretty obvious. First Courtney, then Kaylee. Someone has a problem with us. We're just too moral."

I could think of quite a few other adjectives that described Courtney more accurately, but I had to admit that as far as I could tell, Kaylee had been the real deal. Sure, her perkatude was annoying as could be, but as far as I knew she wasn't anything other than what she'd presented herself to be—a virgin obsessed with the perfect tan and twirling giant colorful flags at football games.

"Has anyone been threatening the Color Guard?" I asked.

Caitlyn nodded. "All the time. We get at least one hate letter a day. Some people just can't stand that we're so good."

Go figure.

"Anyone in particular?" I asked. "Any threats seem especially menacing?"

Caitlyn scrunched up her nose, checking her mental memory banks. "Usually the threats are anonymous. But there was one last week from one of the Goth boys. He yelled 'bitch' at Courtney when we were leaving the Jamba Juice."

Hm. It was a far cry from yelling expletives to strangulation.

I decided to go at it from another angle. "Any idea what Kaylee might have been doing out on the football field at that time of night?"

Caitlyn shook her head. "No. Sorry."

"She didn't mention meeting anyone?"

Again with the head shake. "No."

"When was the last time you talked to Kaylee?"

"Yesterday. After school we went for mani-pedis. You know, to get our minds off Courtney."

"How did she seem then?" Sam asked. "Nervous or upset about anything?"

Caitlyn put her hands on her hips. "You mean other than our best friend being killed?"

"Right. So, where did she go after the spa?" I asked.

"Home. She said she had a lot of chem homework to do." She gave me a pointed look. "Some of us actually pay attention to our science labs."

Yeah, I was gonna have to find out what that blue stuff was.

"And that was the last time you saw her?" I asked.

Caitlyn nodded. Then did a patented non-mascara-smearing sob. "She was such a good friend. I don't know what I'm going to do without her."

Even if her tears never reached her eye makeup, and her grieving process involved spa treatments, this statement I believed. Color Guard girls traveled in packs. And Caitlyn had suddenly been made a lone wolf.

"I'm the only one left now," she said as if reading my thoughts. "Which makes me next."

"Have you received any specific threats?" I asked.

She shook her head. "Isn't the death of both my best friends threat enough?"

Honestly, I probably wouldn't be slinking down any dark alleyways either if I were her.

"Look, I have to get back to work," Caitlyn said, backing

up. "Just stay away from me, 'kay? I'm not ready to die."

I rolled my eyes. "I am not the angel of death."

"Whatevs. You're not much of a good luck charm, either."

She had me there.

When Sam pulled the green machine onto my block to drop me off, I saw that Raley was, predictably, parked outside my house, half a liberally freckled arm hanging out the car window, while Daughtry played at a very low volume from his speakers. Which, in itself, was a sign that he was too old to be listening to Daughtry.

He raised a hand in greeting as Sam dropped me at the curb.

"Hi, Hartley," he said.

I nodded his way.

"Go out after school?"

I nodded again.

"Where?"

I shrugged. "Places."

"To do?"

"Stuff?"

"What kind of stuff?"

"Teenager stuff."

"Nice car," he said, changing tactics. "It makes me hungry."

I had a feeling most things made Raley hungry.

I turned my back to him, walking up the front steps and into the house. I dumped my bag near the bottom of the stairs and wandered into the kitchen. A note greeted me on the kitchen counter:

Hart,
Went to Yogalates class. Grab something from the
freezer for dinner.
P.S. Keep the door locked and don't answer the
phone!

I grabbed a pint of hidden ice cream from the back of the freezer. (Okay, I'll admit the scent of Kevin's car made me hungry, too.) After all, Mom had said to get something from the freezer, and if I ate Chunky Monkey, there was dairy, protein (nuts), and fruit (bananas). That sounded like a balanced meal to me.

I took my dinner and a spoon upstairs and cracked open my homework. But as much as I tried to focus on my chem labs, my mind was somewhere else.

Or, more accurately, fifteen different places, as pieces of information I'd assembled over the last few days floated through my brain in seemingly random patterns. None of it seemed to fit, and yet I felt like everything I needed to figure this out was there.

Scooping more ice cream into my mouth (was there anything better than chocolate and bananas?) I shoved my chem aside and grabbed a Sharpie and a pad of paper.

On cop shows, there were three main things that detectives always looked at—means, motive, and opportunity. I wrote all three down on the pad.

I focused on the first one. In this case, means was a bust. Just about everyone at Herbert Hoover High owned a pair of iPod earbuds. And, while I didn't know exactly what Kaylee had been hit on the back of the head with, the collection of large rocks readily available outside the football field meant it wouldn't have been hard to find a blunt object.

Which left me with opportunity and motive.

Unfortunately, opportunity seemed almost as wide-open as means. So far Andi Brackenridge was the only one we had questioned who had any sort of solid alibi. Plus, she seemed to have more of a motive to keep Courtney alive than dead.

Which left me wondering just who did have a motive for killing Courtney.

Shiloh had said she'd seen Chase going into Josh's house just before Courtney died. If that was true, what motive could Chase possibly have for killing Courtney? They clearly didn't run in the same circles, and I had a hard time seeing Chase as Courtney's type. He was dark and deep. But in a real way, not the way most guys tried to buy an image at Hot Topic. He was the complete antithesis of clean-cut Josh. Surely Courtney would have had zero interest in a guy like Chase.

So what was the connection? Why would Chase possibly want Courtney dead?

I didn't know. But one thing was for sure: It was time to find out if Chase was friend or foe.

SEVENTEEN

THE NEXT DAY WAS SATURDAY, WHICH MEANT (A) NO school, (B) no homework, and (C) the perfect wide-open day to do a little investigating of one brooding bad boy. In lieu of walking up to Chase and calling him out as a killer, Sam and I decided the best way to find out if he had homicidal tendencies was to search his bedroom. If there was any evidence that he'd killed two people, that was the most likely place for it to be.

The only problem was we needed Chase out of said bedroom full of evidence. Luckily, I had a plan.

Sam and I composed an anonymous tip of our own, emailing it to Chase from Kevin's computer:

I know who the killer is. Meet me at Starbucks at 1 p.m.

Chase lived a good ten minutes away from Starbucks (though, the way he drove, I was only budgeting for five), and he'd likely wait at least ten minutes before realizing he'd been stood up, and then it would take him another five minutes to drive back. I figured we had at least twenty solid minutes to search his place.

Once we'd set the stage, Sam and I begged an hour with the green machine from Kevin (we had to promise to bring him back more brownie mix this time), and by 12:50 on the dot, we were pulling onto Beacon Street.

The crime scene tape was gone from Josh's house, though I noticed the lawn was starting to show growth, and the windows were still closed up tight against the warm sun, a sign that his parents had not yet been able to get back from Alaska. While it had only been five days since Courtney's murder, the entire place looked deserted and forlorn. I wondered if it would ever feel the same, considering what had happened within its walls. Personally, if I were Josh, I'd sleep in the living room for the rest of my life rather than spend another night in that bedroom.

Sam and I drove past Josh's place and parked around the corner, just out of sight of Chase's house. We hopped out of the car and took up surveillance behind a sculptured evergreen hedge in the shape of troll doll hair.

I peeked around the bush. Chase's Camaro was still parked in the driveway. He hadn't left yet. I ducked back.

"He's still there," I whispered to Sam.

She nodded. I looked down at my cell readout—12:53.

He was cutting it kind of close.

Either that or he didn't believe the tip was real (good instincts) and was ignoring it altogether.

I was about to go with theory number two and give up when I heard the sound of a car without a muffler starting.

Sam and I peeked around the shrub once more, just in time to see Chase peel out of the driveway. We crouched behind the bush, making ourselves as small as possible as he roared past us. Luckily, he was too engrossed in hammering his gas pedal to the floor (12:58. Seriously—he was going to be there in two minutes? I said a silent prayer for all those on the road with him) to notice two girls trying to blend into the evergreens.

Phase one, a success. Time for phase two of our brilliant plan: getting past Chase's parental units and into his bedroom.

I hid around the side of his house as Sam walked up the steps and knocked on the front door. A moment later it was opened by an older guy with thinning hair and a protruding beer belly.

He gave Sam an expectant look. "Can I help you?" he asked in a deep baritone.

"Uh, hi," Sam answered nervously. "I'm super, super sorry, but . . . is that your car parked at the curb?" she pointed to a sedan parked just to the right of the driveway.

The guy nodded. "Yeah. Why?"

"I think I just hit it with my car."

"What!"

Sam cowered at the guy's loud voice, but I was proud to see her sticking with the story we'd created.

"I don't think I scratched it or anything, but maybe you should come have a look just to be sure?"

"Great," Papa Chase muttered, leaving the porch to follow Sam down the front steps.

As we'd counted on, his entire attention was focused on his precious baby. He didn't even notice the girl slipping around the corner, through the open front door, and into his house.

The TV was on in the living room, a Giants game blaring. I heard sounds in the kitchen like someone was unloading a dishwasher.

I quickly scuttled up the stairs and down the hallway to Chase's bedroom door and slipped inside.

Phase two complete. On to phase three: evidence gathering.

I took a moment to stand behind the closed bedroom door and catch my breath as I looked around. The same band posters greeted me, guys sticking their tongues out and girls dressed in next to nothing hanging off the tongue waggers. The desk was still piled high with camera equipment, but the bed was unmade today, showing off a set of *Star Wars* themed sheets beneath the black comforter. Yeah. *Star*

Wars. I grinned at the small chink in Chase's armor of cool.

I decided to start with the desk, digging into the first drawer. Rubber bands, paper clips, a stapler, and two pads of paper. One had doodles all over the front of little cartoon guys carrying guns of various sizes. Not exactly friendly hearts and rainbows but not necessarily all that different from what any other guy in my class might draw. A scattering of pens minus their matching caps sat off to the side, and a glue stick rounded out the drawer. Nothing that proved Shiloh was right about Chase being the killer.

Then again, nothing that proved she wasn't.

I moved on to the second drawer. This one held a collection of photographs. I raised an eyebrow. Now we were getting somewhere. I grabbed a handful and sifted through them. Most were black-and-white, capturing various architectural shapes and shadows. I was surprised to find a series of portraits among the artsy stuff. The first was of an older guy on a bench at the park. He was sitting alone, his shoulders hunched, a far-off look in his eyes that immediately made me feel nostalgic for some time I'd never actually known. It was a simple scene, but the emotion Chase had captured was surprisingly powerful. I flipped to the next picture. This one was the polar opposite of the first, depicting a small boy on a jungle gym. He was hanging upside down, the look of pure joy on his face so innocent I couldn't help but smile, too. Chase definitely had a gift for capturing a moment.

The click of the front door closing jerked me out of my thoughts. Sam had gotten off the hook, and Daddy was back at his baseball game. I looked down at my cell—1:05. I was on borrowed time.

I put the photos back and crossed to the bookcase on the opposite wall, scanning its contents for anything that screamed "psycho killer."

I tilted my head, reading the titles of the books on his shelf. *Atlas Shrugged, Cannery Row, Catch-22.* I'm not sure what sort of reading material I'd expected to find, but I was impressed. He was a real reader. None of these were on our school assigned reading list.

Beside the paperbacks were a couple of black binders, their covers scratched and showing their cardboard innards at the corners. Clearly well used. I pulled one from the shelf, flipping it open. Handwritten pages filled it, messy, sloping letters covering lined paper. I squinted at the page, trying to read the first one, telling myself that it could possibly be a confession instead of admitting I was just being nosy at this point.

> *When the winter wind whips her hair*
> *Sunshine fills my soul.*
> *When the fall dawn lights her eyes,*
> *The promises of spring bloom in my chest.*

No. Way.

It was a love poem! Who knew Bad Boy had a soft side?

I flipped to the next page. I couldn't help it. It was another poem, this one darker, about a shadow falling over the world. The next one looked like an analogy about waves on the sand obliterating footprints like a new love washing memories of an old one.

I was so engrossed in reading his binder of personal musings that I almost didn't hear the sound outside the window.

Almost.

"Caw! Caw!"

I froze. No. Tell me Sam didn't just . . .

"Caw!"

I crossed to the window, drawing back the black sheet that served as a makeshift curtain. I blinked against the sudden onslaught of light in Midnight Room, looking down. Just below, on the outside of the gate, stood Sam, jumping up and down flapping her arms.

"Caw!"

I opened the window.

"What are you doing?" I hissed.

"Making a bird call to get your attention."

"That is the worst bird sound ever. 'Caw?' What bird actually says that?"

She shook her head, flapping even more violently.

"He's here!" she said.

"He?"

"Chase! He just pulled up and . . ." She spun around. "Oh, eff." And with that she ducked behind a begonia bush.

Uh-oh. Not good.

I briefly contemplated jumping out the window but since (A) I was one story off the ground with no helpful tree next to the house, and (B) it was screened in, that thought was short-lived. Instead, I shoved the binder back on the shelf and quickly scanned the room for somewhere to hide. In the closet? I pulled open the doors. And was greeted by a pile of dirty clothes at least as tall as I was. Ew.

I spun around. Okay, how about the desk? I ducked down onto my hands and knees, but could only fit my butt underneath it, my head still sticking out in the open.

Which left just one more place. Under the bed. God only knew what sort of science experiments lived under a teenaged guy's bed. I paused, trying to think of an alternative.

Then I heard it. A voice on the other side of the door mumbling something, and Chase's voice in response.

"I sent in the paperwork yesterday."

More mumbling.

"I just have the entrance essay left."

His voice was louder this time. In a second, he'd be at the door.

I lifted up his black fuzzy blanket and contemplated

the dark abyss beneath. It was now or never. I took a deep breath, prayed I wouldn't touch anything too gross or, worse yet, living, and crawled on my belly under the bed. My right foot ran into the wall and my left touched something soft and squishy. I stifled a groan. I could detect the mingling scents of pizza and the gym at school. I bit my lip, wondering if maybe the closet wasn't such a bad idea after all.

Only, I didn't get the chance to act on my second-guessing as the door opened and a pair of black boots entered the room. I was pretty sure they were connected to Chase's body, but from my vantage point, they were just shoes.

I watched them cross from the door to the desk and heard the sound of something being deposited on its surface. A backpack fell to the ground, sending a shower of dust bunnies rushing toward me. I held my breath, willing myself not to sneeze. I heard a few more sounds—a couple of clicks, a bumping sound, a tapping. Honestly he could have been playing the drums or constructing a model *Mona Lisa*, I had no idea.

Then the feet were on the move again. They went from the desk, back across the room to the closet doors, pulling them open. I gave myself a little mental pat on the back that I hadn't chosen that as my hiding place after all.

I watched the feet shift and heard the sound of clothing rustling.

Then watched as a black T-shirt hit the ground.

I held my breath. Could it be that I was witnessing Chase undressing?

Okay, I guess I was listening more than witnessing, but it still felt a little wrong.

And a little exciting at the same time.

Bad Hartley. God, I was not interested in seeing Chase naked. I didn't care what sort of six-pack he had hiding under his black T-shirts, even though I was pretty sure it was tight and hot by the way said shirts clung to him.

Oh God. I did want to see him undress.

So badly, in fact, that as a belt fell to the floor, I couldn't help scooting ever so slightly forward, lifting the corner of the *Star Wars* sheet dangling in my face, and peeking around it.

I looked up . . .

. . . and saw that my ears had not deceived me. Chase was, in fact, naked from the waist up.

And he did, in fact, have a six-pack. A really, really nice one. For someone who did his best to avoid any pinprick of sunlight in his room, I had no idea how he got such a nice, even tan. But he did. Warm, honey colored. Except right at the waistband of his jeans where it faded to a pale, smooth color just before his pants gobbled up the rest of my view.

I bit my lip, loath to admit the kind of thoughts that were instantly running through my head. Like, if Josh had a six-pack like that, the chances of my still being a virgin were significantly lower.

I watched as Chase leaned down and undid the laces on his boots, kicking them off to the side. A minute later, he stripped off his socks, too, sending them into the same pile.

And then he did the unthinkable. His hands went to the buttons on his jeans.

Oh, no.

Please, no. Not the pants . . .

Okay, this was bad. I was officially a peeping Tom. Or a peeping Hartley. Or whatever you wanted to call me. But I could not take my eyes off his fingers, slowly undoing the top button of his jeans, giving me my very own private peep show, while I lay with something soft and squicky at my right toe and large dust bunnies tickling my nose.

The button popped open, and I prayed Chase was wearing a pair of really big, baggy boxers.

No such luck. My eyes were glued, as if watching a car wreck, as he slid the zipper down a scant inch.

No boxer waistband.

No tighty-whitey waistband.

Chase was going commando.

"Stop!" I yelled. I covered my eyes with one hand as I crawled out from under the bed.

"Holy . . . !" Chase jumped back a full foot, knocking

into his desk and sending a stack of photos falling to the floor.

"Do not undo that zipper!" I commanded, my hand still over my eyes. (Mostly. Was it bad that I was peeking a little?)

"God, Hartley," Chase muttered. I was glad to hear the sound of a zipper being quickly pulled up, and I uncovered my eyes just as Chase redid his top button, looking self-conscious for the first time since I'd met him. "What are you doing?" he yelled. A vein I hadn't noticed before bulged in the side of his neck.

"Um . . . hiding."

"From?"

"You."

"Why?"

"So you wouldn't know I broke into your bedroom to look for evidence."

Why my brain chose now to start spewing truth, I had no idea. I just wished it would stop soon. And here I'd thought I'd gotten to be a much better liar in the past few days, too.

"Evidence of what?" he asked, narrowing his eyes at me.

"That you killed Courtney and Kaylee."

His eyes went wide with surprise, then narrow again. Really narrow. He crossed his arms over his naked chest. (Which, by the way, made his biceps bulge in a very distracting way.) "You have got to be kidding me."

At that moment, I kinda wished I was.

"Everything okay in there?" I heard from the other side of the door.

"Yeah, Dad. Fine," Chase called. Though the way he was glaring at me through tiny slits of eyes didn't really seem all that fine to me. Apparently he took as liberal use of the word as I did.

"Uh . . . sorry?" I said, though it came out more as a question.

"Sorry? Sorry! God, Hartley, what could possibly have made you think I was the killer?"

I squatted my shoulders. "Someone saw you."

He raised an eyebrow. "Saw me what?"

"Going into Josh's house right after Courtney did."

"They were mistaken."

I shook my head. "No, she was very sure."

"She?" he asked, glomming onto the word. "This wouldn't be Deep Blogger, would it? Shiloh?"

I bit my lip. Then very carefully shook my head in the negative. "No."

"For the love of . . . Hartley, I broke up with her." I guess I wasn't quite as good a liar as I hoped. "She's pissed at me," he continued.

"I said it wasn't her."

He gave me a "get real" look.

"Okay, fine. *Maybe* it was her."

"And *maybe* she told you I killed Courtney out of some sick sense of revenge. Maybe she set up this whole Deep Blogger thing to get back at me."

"She said you broke up with her on Twitter."

Chase ran a hand through his hair. "There was more to it than that. Our relationship was complicated, okay? And, honestly, I couldn't stand another confrontation with her. So, yeah, I ended it. Which is why she's making this stuff up about me now."

"I don't know. She seemed really scared of you."

"She's in drama club. She was acting scared."

"It didn't feel like acting to me. And I know her acting skills. Her snake wasn't that good."

Chase gave me a look. "Snake?"

But before I could explain, he shook his head. "You know what, it doesn't matter. I can tell you for a fact that it wasn't me she was scared of."

"She saw your eagle hoodie."

Chase went to the closet, pulled it open, and grabbed the offending object of clothing. "This one? There are probably dozens of other people at school who have this. It's not exactly one of a kind, you know."

I bit my lip. Good point. I hadn't thought of that.

"Are you sure?" I asked.

"That I'm not a killer? Yeah, pretty sure."

"Sorry." And this time I wholeheartedly meant it. Especially the way the anger had kinda fizzled from his eyes and been replaced with something a whole lot worse. Hurt.

I sucked.

"I'm really, really sorry," I said again. The irony of how very like Josh I sounded at the moment was not lost on me.

Chase opened his mouth to speak, but before he could, a sound erupted from outside.

"Caw! Caw, Hartley, caw!"

Chase narrowed his eyes again. "Sam?"

I nodded. Then crossed to the window again and called down to Sam. "You can quit squawking. He caught me."

"He's not murdering you or anything, is he?"

I glanced at Chase. I couldn't promise the thought hadn't crossed his mind. . . .

"No, I'm fine."

"Oh. Okay, in that case, I'll bring the car around."

"Sam thinks I'm a killer, too?" Chase asked as I pulled my head back from the window.

I nodded. Slowly.

"Great."

"Look, I'm so sor—" I started, but he didn't let me finish.

"Whatever. Just get out of here."

I opened my mouth to say more, but realized that

beyond sorry I didn't really know what to say. So I nodded, and then slunk out of his room with my proverbial
tail between my legs. His dad looked up briefly as I made
my way through the house and out the front door, but he
was too engrossed in the game to care about exactly where
I'd come from.

I closed the front door behind me just as Sam pulled up
with a burger-scented cough.

"Was it my bird call that gave it away?"

I shook my head, relaying the striptease that had busted
my cover as I got in.

"Dude," she said, when I was done.

"I know."

Sam shook her head at me. "I totally would have let
him finish."

"Trust me, I was tempted."

"So, I guess he's not our killer?"

I shrugged. "He says not."

"And you believe him?"

I nodded. "Yeah. Mostly."

"Okay, if the killer isn't Shiloh and it's not Andi and it's
not Chase, then who is it?"

That was the million-dollar question.

EIGHTEEN

RALEY WAS, AS USUAL, PARKED IN FRONT OF MY HOUSE when I got home. I didn't bother with the witty banter. In fact I didn't even give him a second look. He was scenery as far as I was concerned. About as interesting as the azalea shrubs along the sidewalk. I'm not sure he regarded me with the same detached lack of interest, his eyes burning into the back of my head as I unlocked the front door, but at least he didn't get out and chase me down. Thank God for small favors.

But as soon as I walked in the door, I realized I could have used a bigger one.

"Hartley, where have you been?" Mom grabbed me around the middle, doing her boa constrictor imitation again.

"Um, out?" I managed with my last breath.

She released me and did a quick assessment of my person for blunt force trauma. Finding none, her expression did a quick change, concern instantly replaced with anger. Lots of anger.

"Damn it, Hartley, there's a killer out there!"

"Whoa. Did you just swear, Mom?"

She ignored me, shaking her head. "You can't just go 'out.' It's not safe."

"I'm fine, Mom."

"Why didn't you tell me you were leaving the house this morning?"

"I never tell you when I leave the house."

"I was worried sick!"

"I had my cell with me." I pulled it out and looked at the screen. Eighteen missed calls. Oops. "Oh. I guess I had it on silent. Sorry."

"I almost called the police, Hartley!"

"The police are already sitting outside our house."

"You are not," Mom continued, completely ignoring my logic, "to leave this house again without my permission. No going 'out.' No disappearing without notice."

"I didn't disappear—"

"No going *anywhere* without a parent present. Do I make myself clear?"

Crystal.

"Great. Some guy goes on a killing spree and I'm the

one under house arrest."

Mom glared at me. "I'm serious, Hartley."

So was I, but I didn't think now was the time to point that out. Instead, I nodded, doing my best to look like I might actually comply.

Don't get me wrong—most of the time I have no major beef with Mom. Sure, she's soy crazy and a little neurotic, but she's doing her best with the single-mom thing and, honestly, as parents go, could be a whole lot worse. So my act of rebellion at the moment had nothing to do with some deeply rooted need to buck parental authority and everything to do with the fact that (A) a killer was on the loose, and (B) he was systematically ruining my life.

Fleetingly I wondered if that was the killer's real motive—to crush Hartley's social life one small step at a time—but even I wasn't self-absorbed enough to really believe it. Instead, I had to nod at Mom and listen to her say how "totally serious" she was about a hundred more times while she served me a faux BLT (bulgar, lettuce, and tomato), before she finally let me escape to my room.

I opened the door, flipped on the light . . .

And screamed.

Sitting in the middle of my bed, looking like death warmed over, was Josh. He jumped up at the sound of my screech.

Apparently, so did Mom.

"Hartley? Are you okay?" Mom called. I could hear her taking the stairs two at a time.

"Fine! Sorry I . . . stepped on a staple. Ouch."

"Oh." The elephant thumping up the stairs stopped. "Okay. You need a Band-Aid or something?"

"Nope. I'm fine. Thanks." I quickly shut the door behind me.

"What are you doing here?" I hissed at Josh.

"I didn't mean to scare you," he said, giving me a sheepish grin. "I just . . . I've run out of places to go."

While my heart rate had slowed from crack addict levels, it was still hovering in the fifty Red Bulls region. I took a couple deep breaths to slow it down while I got a good look at Josh. It had been only three days since I'd last seen him, but the difference was noticeable. Being on the run was a hard life. He had dark circles under his eyes as if he hadn't been able to rest, knowing the entire San José police force was after him. He had a fine sprinkling of stubble along his jaw that seemed completely at odds with his boy-next-door looks, and his clothes were wrinkled and kinda gray. And they didn't smell too hot either.

"Where have you been hiding out?" I asked, sitting on the bed. Though not too close. (Did I mention the stench?)

"Here and there. I slept in the park last night."

Like a homeless person? As much as I hated him for everything that had happened in the last week, I suddenly felt ridiculous for thinking my life was being ruined. At least I had a warm bed and endless home-cooked soy meals.

"You hungry?" I asked. "We have . . . soy?"

He gave me a small smile that didn't quite reach his eyes. "I'll pass. But thanks."

"Sure."

Silence hit us then. Thick. Heavy. Pregnant with all the stuff that I'd yelled at him the other night. All the stuff that he'd done behind my back before that.

"So . . ." he finally said, "are you close to finding him yet?"

"Him?"

"The killer?"

I bit my lip. I hated to tell him that for all our investigating, Sam and I weren't really all that much closer than we had been to begin with. Sure, we'd muddied the waters plenty, but actually catching the killer? Not so much.

"Kinda," I said instead.

"Really?" His eyes lit up, bright and hopeful in stark contrast to his disheveled appearance. I fought down another wave of sympathy. He was cheating, lying scum. I was not going to feel sympathetic toward him. No matter how pathetic and alone he was now.

"We've got a few suspects," I hedged.

"Who?"

I bit my lip again. "I'd rather not say until we narrow things down a little more." I half expected my nose to grow to Pinocchio lengths with that statement.

Luckily, Josh was nowhere near as good as Chase at seeing through my half-truths. Instead, he said, "That's good news. Really good news."

There was a pause again.

"I really appreciate this, Hartley," he said, his voice low and thick with emotion. "You're all I have left. Look, Hart, I—"

"Don't," I said automatically. I was having a hard enough time stomping down the sympathy any normal person would feel for a lonely, scared guy on the run. I couldn't deal with throwing our complicated relationship into the mix, too. I was focused on finding out who had killed Courtney and Kaylee. That was it. Dead bodies I could deal with. My feelings toward my ex-boyfriend? I was still a little too chicken to delve too deeply into those.

But Josh didn't back down so easily.

"Please listen. This may be the only chance I get to say this."

I took a deep breath, reminded myself he was pond scum, and steeled myself to hear the worst. "Fine. What?"

He licked his lips. "I was wrong. I hurt you, and I can never tell you how sorry I am. I know I can't take it back, even though I would do anything to," he said, leaning forward. "I really would. These last few days, I've had a lot of time to think, and, Hartley, I just want you to know that I realize how much I hurt you. I betrayed your trust. And I will never forgive myself."

That was by far the most intelligent thing I had ever heard Josh say. What do you know, being on the run had made him grow up. And grow a soul. A really deep, articulate one.

I stared at a spot of lint on my comforter, blinking back a piece of dust in my eye. (Yes, dust. It was not tears. I had allergies. Probably from having hidden under Chase's bed. No way were they tears, and no way did they mean I had any feelings whatsoever for Josh.)

"Hart," he went on, his voice lower as he leaned forward. "Is there any way that we could possibly start over . . . ? I mean, I know we can't go back to where we were. But maybe we could go forward?"

I blinked hard (Freakin' dust!) and took a deep breath that was surprisingly shaky. I opened my mouth to answer.

Only I never got the chance.

"Freeze!"

My bedroom door flew open so hard it rattled on its hinges, the doorknob denting the wall behind it. Two armed police officers burst through, both holding menacing black guns straight-armed in front of them.

I screamed again. And despite their suggestion to

freeze, I couldn't help instinctively jumping off the bed and scrambling as far into the back wall away from those guns as I could go.

Luckily for my inability to freeze, the police weren't so much interested in me as they were the guy still sitting on my bed like a deer in the headlights.

"Hands over your head!" the first cop shouted at Josh.

Josh complied, shooting both up as high as they could go.

"Don't shoot. Please, God, I didn't kill anyone. Don't shoot!" he pleaded, his voice rising two octaves.

"Josh DuPont?" a familiar voice asked. I looked up from the shiny black guns (With difficulty. Amazing how deadly weapons in your bedroom tend to draw your attention.) to find the round frame of Detective Raley filling my doorway. Behind him, Mom hovered, her hand over her mouth in shock.

"Are you Josh DuPont?" Raley asked again.

Josh nodded, his Adam's apple bobbing nervously up and down, his hands still high above his head.

Raley crossed the room in one quick stride, pulling a pair of handcuffs from his belt and clamping Josh's hands behind his back. "Josh DuPont, you're under arrest for the murders of both Courtney Cline and Kaylee Clark. You have the right to remain silent."

Josh looked at me, fear and pleading in his eyes.

I looked at the black guns again, wishing the cops would holster them already.

And Raley looked like the cat that ate the canary and all his friends, a gleam of satisfaction lighting his eyes, a smirk creasing his freckled cheeks. All those hours of watching my inert front door had finally paid off. Raley had got his man.

NINETEEN

LAST YEAR MY MOM SURPRISED ME FOR MY BIRTHDAY WITH tickets to see *Legally Blonde* the musical up in San Francisco. I'd never seen the movie, but it sounded like fun—bubbly blond, lots of cool costumes, and a day out with Mom in SF. Cool.

I had fallen in love with the musical. Elle Woods was this totally cute, totally fun girl who was actually super-smart underneath it all. An upbeat person who everyone underestimated. It was a classic don't-judge-a-book-by-its-cover story.

Elle became my new hero.

Which is why I felt so stupid when I realized that Raley had pulled an Elle on me. With his typical cop looks, donut-guzzling belly, and fatherly demeanor, I had pegged him as a dumb cop on the wrong track. It turns out he'd actually been a pretty smart cop on the wrong track.

Of course he'd followed me to the football field the night Kaylee died. Of course he realized I must have climbed out my bedroom window. And, of course, he realized that if I could climb out, Josh could easily climb in. In fact, it turns out he'd watched Josh climb in on Wednesday night as well, only he'd been waiting for arrest warrants to come through, so he could be certain that once he picked Josh up, he wasn't going to lose him again. Turns out, you can't legally hold a suspect unless you charge him with something. At least, that's what Cody Banks texted to Jessica Hanson the following morning, explaining what Josh's parents had been told by their high-priced attorney who, despite the $50,000 (or $75,000 depending on whether you believed Kyle's text or Erin Carter's) retainer they'd given him upon returning from Alaska last night, had been unable to get Josh out on bail. So, until his trial date Josh was residing in the Santa Clara County juvenile detention facility.

And by Monday morning, his arrest had once again put yours truly front and center on the tongues (and mobile devices) of the gossip-minded at HHH.

To be honest, by this point I was so used to being the HHH leper that I hardly even cared. In fact, I didn't mind the gossip. I was totally fine with it.

I was fine with the way I could hear my name whispered

a dozen times as I walked down the hall. Hey, it meant everyone knew my name. Look at how popular I suddenly was! The sidelong looks and pointing from across the quad? I was turning heads. Isn't that what every girl wants? And the way conversation stopped every time I walked into the room? Made it that much easier to hear my own thoughts. It was all totally fine.

I was sure that in another week some other tragedy, like Cole Perkins's enormous zit right before homecoming, would capture everyone's collective attention and the Girl Who Dated Killers and Found Dead Bodies would be a thing of the past. Until then, I was so freakin' fine being the star of HHH tabloid texts it wasn't even funny.

So engrossed in my fineness was I that as I rounded the corner to the east wing I almost smacked right into the polyester-clad form of Mary Bessie.

"Hartley," she said, tilting her head ninety degrees to the left. "How are you, dear?"

I took a deep breath.

"Fine."

"You can feel fine, but fine is not a feeling."

I opened my mouth to tell her how fine my feelings were and what a load of crap that was.

But what came out instead was a choked sob.

"It's true. I do have feelings!"

"Oh, honey," she said, enveloping me in a hug that

smelled like patchouli oil and Fancy Feast. "Let it out. Let it all out."

For once, I did as I was told. I hiccupped another big sob. "I don't want Josh to be sorry! I'm not a CSI! I hate being a leper!"

I was aware that I was making no sense. But, thankfully, it seemed that Ms. Bessie was either used to incoherent teens or just didn't much care so long as I was doing the requisite crying.

"Come into my office," she said, putting an arm around me. "I have tea."

"Okay." I sniffed. "I like tea." What can I say? My life had crumbled to the point where all it took to break me was the offer of chamomile brewed on a hot plate.

I followed her down the hall and into a room next to the janitor's closet. It was small, just large enough for a desk, a couple of chairs, and a bookcase filled, I noticed, with volumes on psychology and cat care. A hanging plant was precariously balanced from the ceiling tiles in the corner. I had to hand it to Ms. Bessie for trying to make a former storeroom seem homey and inviting.

On her desk sat a collection of tchotchkes—a PEZ dispenser shaped like an elephant, a Beanie Baby, a pencil holder that looked like a hobbit, and a picture frame decorated with multicolored buttons glued onto Popsicle sticks.

"Your baby?" I asked, pointing to the frame.

"Yes!" Her face lit up with a big smile that showed off two rows of crooked teeth. She flipped the frame around so that I could see the picture. A Volkswagen Beetle with a large tabby cat sitting on the hood.

"Her name is Priscilla. She's my pride and joy. My little fur baby," she said, making kissy faces at the photo.

And *I* was the one who needed counseling?

"She's . . . cute."

"Thanks. I find that felines make great companions. They love you unconditionally even if you don't make the most money in the world and prefer to help young people with their problems instead of becoming the doctor your mother always dreamed of."

"Uh-huh." Suddenly, I felt a whole lot better about my life.

The phone on her desk rang.

"I'm so sorry. Let me just take this then we can chat," Ms. Bessie said. She grabbed the receiver with a cheerful "Mary Bessie here" that was almost done in song. She paused as she listened to the caller on the other end. "Well, when did she last take her meds?" she asked. Another pause. "Some side effects are normal," she went on.

I tuned her out and concentrated on sipping my tea. It was hot and strong, having simmered on the hot plate at the edge of her desk since God knows when. I took another sip. I had to admit, it did have a bit of a comforting effect.

The warm liquid flowing down my throat somehow cleansed the taste of tears away. And as it hit my belly, it calmed the anxiety bubble that had taken root ever since guys with guns had burst into my bedroom on Saturday night. And the heat of the cup against my palms was nice. Warm was a good feeling. One that was tangible, identifiable. Safe. Unlike the thousand different unidentifiable feelings warring in my belly when I thought of Josh, Raley, Chase, and this whole mess I'd gotten myself into.

Yes, I had feelings. And they were not fine. They were a freaking mess. To be honest, I wasn't sure what I'd been about to say to Josh when Raley and his goons had burst in. The look in his eyes, the sincerity in his voice . . . I mean, we all make mistakes, right? Sure, some of them are larger and more deadly than others, but the thought of Josh in a prison cell had left me tossing and turning all weekend.

Not to mention the fact that the police arresting a guy for murder on my bed had made my mom freak out so badly she'd called my dad and they'd spent the next two hours tag-team lecturing me on speakerphone about how I would never be allowed to look at a guy again until I was thirty, let alone date. And having my own car? No way. Going away to college and living in a dorm? *Way* too risky. At one point Mom even suggested having me implanted with a homing chip, and Dad actually considered it for a moment before telling me I was officially grounded until the end of my natural life. Or until I turned eighteen, whichever came first (and judging by the way he was growling at me, it was a toss-up).

And, as if that weren't enough, Chase had texted me.

You lied to me.

As soon as the cops had left, and I was free from the Lecture to End All Lectures, I had called Sam and told her everything, still shaking as I recalled the gleaming black of *real* guns pointed at me and the click of Josh's handcuffs. Of course, Sam had immediately called Kyle, who had texted half the water polo team, and in an hour's time, everyone on the Verizon network knew.

Including Chase.

The truth was, I'd lied to a lot of people in the past week. As much as I'd been pissed at Josh for lying to me, I'd turned around and become what I'd hated him for. Granted, I hadn't professed my undying love to Chase, then gotten naked with some guy behind his back. But I had promised him my partnership. And I had hid Josh from him. I was pretty sure he knew I'd been hiding Josh the whole time, but I guess the confirmation was the difference between wondering what a condom wrapper was doing in your boyfriend's locker and seeing video footage of him with Courtney Cline behind the bassoon rack.

I'd spent all Saturday night plagued by disturbing

dreams of people chanting "liar, liar, pants on fire," Josh's puppy dog eyes, Chase driving at a breakneck speed away from me in his dented Camaro, and Courtney Cline's puffy face, her tongue protruding from her mouth as she asked me why I couldn't find her justice.

I took another sip of chamomile.

But the tea would make it all better.

I glanced again at the picture of Priscilla. Maybe I should get a cat. I could dig being a crazy cat lady. Priscilla looked nice. Nonjudgmental. Maybe Ms. Bessie was onto something here.

I looked at the picture. Sipped my chamomile. Looked at the cat on the hood of the car again. It was one of those older Beetles that you hardly ever see on the road anymore, most having broken down in surrender sometime during the seventies. But it was cute. Distinctive, kinda like Ms. Bessie.

I took another sip of tea, wondering what kind of car I might have gotten if I hadn't been grounded until the end of time. What car would fit me? A cute Beetle? A sporty Jeep like Josh's? A speedy little Camaro like Chase's?

And suddenly it hit me.

Sam and I had borrowed a car to drive to Josh's house after school. With such a short window of time, the killer must have driven to Josh's house as well, if he'd gotten there before us. No way could he have had time to walk there from school, kill Courtney, and leave before we pulled up.

Which meant he had to have a car.

Which meant he had to have parked it somewhere on Josh's street.

I popped up from my seat, making for the door.

"Hartley?" Ms. Bessie called. "Where are you going?" she asked, covering the phone receiver with one hand.

"I'm great. You know what, that tea totally worked." I looked down. In my haste, I'd almost walked out with her "Feelings Are Our Friends" mug. I set it down on her desk. "Thanks. I feel ten times better. You are so good at your job," I said, waving behind me as I backpedaled out the door.

"Oh. Well, okay . . . I guess," she said, waving after me.

The second I was free, I dug my phone from my book bag, ignoring the bell echoing off the walls, signaling the end of first period. People rushed by me on both sides, running to their next classes as I typed in Chase's number. I impatiently tapped my foot against the linoleum floor as it rang three times on the other end. I swear I could feel him reading the screen on his end and mentally debating whether or not he wanted to take a call from a total liar. Apparently, he went with not, as the call was tossed to his voice mail. But I was hot on an idea to bust this case wide open, and I was not going to be deterred by voice mail. I dialed again. This time he picked up on the second ring.

"What?"

I swallowed down the lump of regret and glossed over the less than friendly greeting.

"I need to see your pictures again. The ones you took the day of Courtney's murder."

I could feel him frowning on the other end. "Why?"

"There may be evidence in them. Where are you? Can we meet at your place?"

"I'm not sure I'm comfortable having you there."

Okay, I deserved that.

I took a deep breath. "I'm sorry I lied, I like your *Star Wars* sheets, you're not that bad of a driver, and I swear on my new Very Cherry lip gloss that I will never lie to you again."

I thought I heard a muffled laugh on the other end, but when his voice came back it was as deadpan as ever. "What evidence?"

I took that as a good sign.

"The killer had to have driven to Josh's house, which means his car must have been parked nearby while he was killing Courtney."

"Okay . . ." he hedged.

"And, by the time Sam and I got there, he was gone."

"Which means, his car would be, too," Chase said. I could feel his mental gears clicking into rotation.

"Which means," I said, "we need to look at the pictures

and see which car was on the street at two thirty—"

"And gone by three fifteen!"

"Exactly!"

"I'm on it. I've got the pictures on my camera at home. I'll ditch my next class and go look them up."

"Text me as soon as you find something."

"Done," he said, and hung up.

Whether it was the chamomile or the good long cry or the fact that Chase was once again speaking to me, I had a little spring in my step as I walked to second period, only five minutes late. I might be a leper, but I was a leper with a clue.

TWENTY

I WAS ALMOST GLAD TO HAVE P.E. SECOND PERIOD SO that I could burn off my excess energy. Though, I had to admit, I was totally preoccupied during volleyball with listening for my phone to ring from my bag on the bench. So preoccupied that I got hit in the head by a spike. Twice. After the second time Coach Chapin took pity on me and let me sit out.

At the end of the period, I stood beside my locker and stared at my phone for a full minute and a half, willing it to buzz to life with news from Chase. No such luck. I was still willing with all my might when a familiar voice hailed me from down the hall.

"Hartley? Hartley Grace Featherstone? Can I have a minute?"

I looked up to find Diane Dancy bearing down on me,

her intern and cameraman in tow.

I did a quick look left, then right for any means of escape, but she had me cornered against banks of lockers on both sides. And before I could slip past her, the little red light on the camera was lit, the lens was pointed my way, and Diane was shooting rapid-fire questions my way.

"What was it like watching the police arrest your boyfriend for murder?" she asked, shoving a microphone in my face. "Has he contacted you? Will you be at his trial? Is he still claiming innocence?"

I blinked at her, trying to decide which question to answer first. "Um . . ."

"How does it feel to know that your boyfriend is in jail?"

"*Ex*-boyfriend" I clarified, looking past her to see a crowd of people gathering in the hall. "And he's innocent," I added, as much for her benefit as theirs.

"Of course he's yet to be proven guilty in a court of law," Diane conceded.

I shook my head. "No, I mean he really is innocent. Everything we've uncovered so far points to the fact that someone is framing him."

Diane took a step forward. "So, you're still investigating?"

I nodded. "Yes. In fact, we're very close to finding the real killer."

She grinned, giving me a patronizing look. "The police believe the *real* killer is already in custody."

"Well, they're wrong," I said. Then added, "And I can prove it."

"You can?"

"Well . . . I will be able to. Soon. We have a very strong lead that we're currently pursuing."

Diane nodded, though whether she actually believed me or not, I'd be hard-pressed to say. "Your loyalty to your boyfriend is very admirable."

"*Ex*-boyfriend," I said again. Though the camera had already swiveled away from me and back to Diane, who was informing the viewing public they should watch at eleven for the latest updates on "the Herbert Hoover High killer awaiting the swift hand of justice" behind bars.

Oh, brother.

I quickly slipped past her and navigated the crowd of students suddenly all texting each other about crazy Hartley's latest Nancy Drew moment. Not that I cared. At the moment, I had a one-track mind, and it was stuck on waiting for word from Chase.

Which, by the way, did not come during third period, despite the fact that I checked my phone every five minutes. What was taking him so long? How hard was it to compare a few pictures and spot which one of these things didn't belong? By the end of fourth, I was a wreck. I would have ditched school and driven to Chase's house myself if I'd had a car. And wasn't grounded for the rest of my natural life.

Finally, five minutes before lunch, my phone buzzed to life in my pocket, the jolt making me jump in my seat. Luckily, Senorita Gonzalez didn't notice as I slipped it out of my jeans and checked the readout.

Unluckily, it was not from Chase.

A number came up, but it wasn't one I had programmed into my contacts, so I had no idea who it was. It was local, though, which made me check the text, despite the eagle eyes of Gonzalez roving the classroom.

its andi b.

I read the first line, eliminating that mystery.

i know who killed cc.

I raised an eyebrow. I'd heard this song and dance before. Shiloh had thought she knew who the killer was, too. I was about to discount it when the phone buzzed in my hand again.

i have video. meet me at midnite. ftbal fld.

What was it with people and midnight? Part of me wanted to text back and tell her to cut the drama and just spill who did it. I mean, if Andi really had video, why didn't she show it to me before? Why hadn't she said anything? Was this some sort of new blackmail attempt? If she thought I was willing to pay for info about who killed

Courtney, she had clearly overestimated the amount of my allowance.

On the other hand . . . on the other hand, I honestly felt *this* close to blowing this whole thing wide open. The killer couldn't hide forever. Someone must have seen something. And if Andi had been blackmailing Courtney, maybe she was that someone. Maybe she'd caught something in her blackmail video that, like me with the cars, she hadn't realized was relevant until now.

So, even though I was so over the whole cloak-and-dagger thing, I texted back.

i'll b there.

By the time Sam, Kyle, and I had finished our pizza sticks and wilted Caesar salads from the cafeteria, I still hadn't heard from Chase. I couldn't take the silence anymore, so I shot off a text.

whats takin so long?

Almost immediately, my phone rang in response, Chase's name lighting up the screen.

"Dude, where are you?" I asked.

"*Dude*, I'm checking the pictures."

"For the last four hours?"

He sighed. "I had to enlarge them all to see the details. Most of the pics only have a corner of the street visible here and there anyway. And I took like a hundred of them. It's taking some time to compare them all."

I resisted the urge to whine like a two-year-old. "How much time?"

"God, you sound like a whiny toddler."

Okay, I *almost* resisted.

"I'll keep looking," Chase assured me, "and you'll be the first to know when I find something."

"Fine," I said, "but hurry!" Then I hung up.

"No killer yet?" Sam asked, making slurping sounds as she sucked up the last of her grape juice.

I shook my head. On the plus side, I had high hopes for my meeting with Andi later. One way or another, we were smoking this guy out tonight.

The second school let out, I realized that my status as the HHH leper was becoming solidified for life. Mom was sitting at the curb in her beige minivan, waiting for me. Listening to Guns N' Roses. At top volume.

"Uh, is that your mom?" Cody Banks asked, coming up behind me.

My face turned beet red, and I'm pretty sure I shrank at least two inches. "No."

"You sure?" he asked, grinning. "'Cause she's waving you over."

"Must be some sort of twitch. I've never seen her before in my life."

I waited until Cody left, then quickly scuttled to the van before anyone else could see me. I pulled open the passenger-side door and slid down so that only the top of my hair was visible through the window.

"Drive! Now!"

Mom shot me a look. "Nice to see you, too, Hartley."

"Uh-huh. Nice. Totally nice. Now go!"

Luckily, she might be dense, but she did have a heart. She drove. And even turned the radio down to a normal volume.

Once we made it home (only three screeching songs later), Mom ushered me into the kitchen, where she proceeded to stir a large pot.

"Set your backpack down. Food's almost ready."

"I'm not hungry," I protested, checking my cell readout for the umpteenth time. Nada.

"You need food," Mom said. "You need to keep your strength up during this trying time."

I rolled my eyes.

"And don't roll your eyes," Mom said, wagging a wooden spoon at me.

"Fine. What are you cooking?"

"Chili."

"It smells like dog food."

"Soy chili."

"Swell."

"Try it." She shoved the spoon in my face.

Reluctantly I nibbled a bite off the end.

"It tastes like dog food."

"Well then, eat up, Fido, 'cause that's what we're having."

"Fine." Geez, what was with the attitude? You'd think it was all my fault I was under police surveillance or something.

I choked down a bowl of chili (which, if I held my breath, was almost palatable), then begged off more "strength" food with homework. Only Mom insisted I do it in the living room, where she could keep a close eye on me.

"What, you don't trust me?"

"Not as far as I could throw you."

"You know, with all the Yogalates you've been doing, I bet you could actually throw me pretty far."

"Nice try. Homework in the living room."

It was almost dark before I was finally allowed to go to my room. And even then, I noticed that an alarm had been attached to my window.

I had a feeling that I might actually be under more sur-veillance at the moment than Josh was.

Which presented a small problem: How to get out to meet Andi?

"How am I going to get out to meet Andi?" I asked

Sam half an hour later after I'd run through every possible scenario of escape. All of which ended with me getting caught.

"You're asking *me*?" Sam laughed. "Dude, if I ever tried to sneak out, you know my dad would kill me. Then ground me. Then maybe kill me again."

Good point. In the five years I'd known Sam, she'd never snuck out after dark. In fact, I was pretty sure she didn't even leave the house after dark, her parents being afraid of what kind of non-Stanford-type behavior might go on among teenagers once the sun went down.

"Maybe you could try the window?"

"Locked. And fitted with an alarm."

"Dude."

"I know."

"Okay, how about this . . . wait until she goes to sleep, then just sneak out the front door."

"She doesn't go to bed until after one. I need to meet Andi at midnight."

"So, sneak out the back door? She can't watch both at once, can she?"

"The backyard floodlights are on. I'd be a sitting duck as soon as I stepped outside."

I heard Sam sigh on the other end and pictured her bangs flying upward. "Sorry, that's all I got. You've reached the limits of my sneakiness."

"Thanks anyway."

"Lemme know how it turns out, okay?"

I nodded at my empty room. "Will do." Then I hung up and dialed another number. While Sam might score a three on the sneaky scale, I had a pretty good idea that someone else I knew was at least an eleven.

"Not done yet" was the greeting Chase gave as he picked up the phone. "Sorry, I had to go back to school to meet with the paper's adviser, then had to edit tomorrow's copy, then there was dinner with the fam. But I'm almost there now. Just going through the last few pics."

Good to know.

"Actually I need your help with something else," I said. Then I told him about my meeting with Andi.

"I'm going with you," Chase said when I was done.

"No!"

"Remember what happened last time?"

All too well.

"Look, Andi is harmless. And no one else knows I'm meeting her. It's perfectly safe."

He paused. "I'm almost done here. I'll follow you and hide. She won't even know I'm there."

"No. I'm fine."

"Too late. It's a done deal. I'll follow you with or without your permission."

I bit my lip. If Andi was going to all this trouble to

meet privately, I was pretty sure she wouldn't appreciate an audience. "Fine," I said. "I'm meeting her at one a.m." I held my breath, closed my eyes, and crossed my fingers.

"Great. I'll be there at one."

I let out a silent breath, thanking the gods of lies that for once I'd been able to pull one over on him. If I were lucky, by one a.m., I'd be safely tucked in my bed and the killer would be on his way to Raley's jail.

"Fine. Now, how am I going to get out of here?" I asked.

He was quiet on the other end for a moment, contemplating his options.

"Your mom is downstairs?" he asked.

"Yep."

"Okay, if she's down, you should go up."

I looked up at my ceiling. "Meaning . . . ?"

"You have an attic?"

I shrugged. "I guess so," I answered. "There's a hole in the ceiling in the laundry room."

"Okay, so climb into the attic, then find the vent, and get out that way."

"Out onto . . . ?"

"I dunno. The roof? You figure it out. I gotta go so I can finish checking the photos."

And he hung up on me.

I stared at the silent phone. He made it sound so easy.

Just climb out onto the roof. Clearly he'd never been a girl with a precarious sense of balance and a slight fear of heights.

However, he had a point. Mom would not be expecting me to go out that way.

I spent the next two hours trying to come up with another way. Unfortunately by 11:15, no lightning bolt of genius had struck me. Up and out it was.

I threw on a pair of old jeans, a black hoodie, and some sneakers, and made for the bedroom door. I cracked it open and stuck my head out.

I could hear Mom watching TV, strains of her DVR'd *The Biggest Loser* filtering up the stairs. I glanced down the hallway. At the very end, near her bedroom, sat the laundry room.

I quickly scuttled from my room, half expecting laser alarms to trip as I passed her bedroom. Luckily, Mom hadn't gone that far (yet), and I made it to the laundry room without incident. I carefully slid in and closed the door behind me.

So far so good.

I looked up at the rectangular cutout in the ceiling above the washing machine. I'd never been up there. Call me crazy, but I wasn't a particularly big fan of dark, creepy places. I hopped on top of the washing machine, cringing at the sound of the metal creaking, and stretched up, pushing the rectangle, sorta expecting nothing to happen.

It gave way easily, sliding up and over to reveal a big black hole.

I stood up straight, my head poking into the attic. More blackness. I took out my phone and opened it. The display cast a bluish glow, allowing me to see wooden beams stretched out over a sea of pink insulation. To the right sat a collection of boxes labeled "Christmas Decorations." To the left, a couple of broken chairs and a dresser missing three drawers. And straight ahead was a metal vent, just a hair larger than I was, a thin strip of moonlight visible through the slats telling me that Chase was indeed correct about it offering a way out.

I should never have doubted his nefarious nature.

I set my phone down on the nearest beam, letting the blue light fill the room as I balanced my hands on the lip of the ceiling for leverage and jumped. Two tries later I had enough upper arm strength to pull myself up into the attic. Once there, I carefully replaced the rectangle of ceiling below me, covering any evidence of my escape route.

It also served to effectively cut my visibility in half, forcing me to completely rely on my cell to light the beam in front of me, though it didn't quite afford enough light to hit the corners of the attic.

I had given up believing in the boogeyman when I was seven. But, if he really did exist and all Mom's lies about him being imaginary were for naught, I had a feeling he probably lived in one of the corners of our attic. They were dark, full of cobwebs, and totally creepy. I put mental blinders on, focusing on the round vent on the far wall gable.

Praying I didn't disturb a nest of spiders (which was right next to heights on the list of things I loved), I hopped from beam to beam, avoiding stepping in the squishy pink insulation. One painstaking step at a time, I finally made it across the room to the vent. I could feel cool air coming in from the outside. A good sign.

I pushed, testing just how sturdy it was. It wiggled. I shoved. It wiggled again but didn't budge. I balanced on one foot on the wooden beam and kicked. This time a corner came loose. I repeated the procedure, hoping that Mom didn't hear the noise. Or just figured we had very big rats. On my second try the vent tilted outward, making a clanging sound that echoed through the attic. I froze, holding my breath, praying the next sound I heard wasn't Mom, investigating.

One second.

Two.

By four Mississippi, I decided she hadn't heard it, and I was safe.

I peeked out the vent opening. Below me was the roof of the garage.

I pushed my head and shoulders through the vent hole, the splintered wood scraping off against my hoodie as I squeezed through. I hunched my shoulders as much as I could, finally getting one arm out to brace myself on the roof below as I wriggled out the other arm, a hip, and one leg. Finally both feet slid out, hitting the shingles.

I took a deep breath, again freezing for the requisite four Mississippi to make sure Mom hadn't heard.

So far so good.

As long as I didn't look down.

Which, of course, was the first thing I did.

Holy effing . . .

That was a long way to fall. I watched the ground kind of sway in front of my eyes, the asphalt of my driveway looking particularly hard and bone breaky from this vantage point. I took a deep breath, told myself to *really* not look down this time, and carefully replaced the vent.

Or tried to. It kinda hung askew, but I figured Mom wasn't about to come inspect the roofline tonight. I turned.

And felt my foot slip on the shingles.

I quickly sat down on my butt, adrenaline rushing through me. I took a couple more deep breaths, then scooted to the edge of the roof. The top of Mom's minivan was two feet below me.

I slid until I was as close as I could get, said a silent prayer, willing all my worldly possessions to Sam if I didn't make it, and jumped.

I landed with a thud on the top of the mom mobile, grateful for once for its big, blocky shape.

I slid on my belly to the back of the car and climbed down feetfirst over the spare tire, never having been so grateful in my life to feel my feet hit the ground. I took a moment to catch my breath, looking around the empty street as I crouched behind the car.

For once, Raley was *not* parked by our front curb. In fact, the entire street was eerily deserted. The lone window lit up was our living room's, where Mom was keeping vigil over her stumbling-upon-dead-bodies-prone daughter, or so she thought.

As I looked back at the house, I had a moment of guilt for sneaking out on her. But just a moment. Hey, she'd made me eat dog-food chili. I think we were even.

I turned my back on the window, ducking my head and setting off down the street.

It was time to see a blackmailer about a video.

TWENTY-ONE

I JOG WALKED THE ENTIRE WAY TO SCHOOL, A STRONG sense of déjà vu washing over me as I passed one empty shop after another, dark storefronts and vacant parking lots signaling that all good people were home in bed at this hour. Part of me wished I was, too, but unless I wanted to spend the rest of my life under house arrest, "good" was something I couldn't afford to be tonight. Instead, I slunk through the night, going over my plan once more.

It was simple: I would look at the video Andi had. If it was any good, I'd call Sam, who, after much pleading, had already convinced Kevin to come pick me and Andi up, and we'd all go straight to the police station, where someone would drag Raley out of bed. (Hey, it was the least I could do, considering he'd burst into my bedroom, gun drawn—dramatic much?—Saturday night.) Then he'd arrest the bad guy, and Kevin would drive me back home before Mom even knew I was gone.

It was a good plan. A solid plan. One that of course depended on Andi actually having some incriminating footage of the killer. But on the off chance that she was either (A) blowing smoke, or (B) trying her hand at some new sort of blackmail scheme, the plan was even simpler: tell her to go to Hades and hightail it home before Mom realized I was gone. (You'll notice that both plans involved Mom never knowing I had snuck out. Very important to the success of either. And my future happiness.)

By the time I reached Main Street, I was feeling confident. I slipped around the mausoleum-looking main building to the back of the school, where I passed a line of portables. While they were supposed to be temporary classrooms, anyone who had grown up in the California school system knew the trailers were the most permanent temporary structures around. I was pretty sure ours predated MTV. I skirted the pool, where the Wildcats practiced water polo, and made my way out to the football field beyond.

Which was, predictably at this hour, deserted. I looked down at my cell—11:47. I was early. I shoved my hands into the front pocket of my hoodie and sat down on the metal bleachers to wait for Andi.

I closed my eyes, listening to the quiet night. An owl

hooted at the far edge of the field. Sprinklers in the quad went off. The hum of the freeway in the distance rumbled behind me.

A loud beeping filled the air, making me jump so high I almost fell off the bleachers.

My cell calling out from my pocket. I took a deep breath. Good thing I wasn't jumpy tonight or anything.

I pulled my phone from my pocket, fully expecting Andi's number to light up my screen, telling me she was a no-show. (This was totally the last time I agreed to meet someone with mysterious info at midnight. Couldn't anyone be mysterious at a reasonable hour?) However, instead of Andi's number, it was Chase's that came up. I flipped my phone open. He'd sent me a picture message.

I scrolled down and read the text:

got it! b4 n after. check whats missing.

Beneath the text two pictures were attached. The first was half a frame of the bumper of Chase's car with a corner of the street behind. I could make out a white truck and a silver sedan. I eagerly moved on to the second photo. I squinted down at the image. Again, Chase's bumper was visible, this time from a different angle, lower, looking up at the dent. The background was slightly out of focus, but I could make out the same stretch of street as the first picture, the truck again parked at the curb. Only in this one the sedan was missing.

I felt my pulse quicken. This was it! I checked the corner of the photos for a time stamp. I longed for a nice big computer monitor, but I held the phone up, squinting at the corner. The first one read 2:34. The second 3:17. The time fit perfectly. The sedan owner had to be our killer!

I looked more carefully. Unfortunately, the pictures showed nothing of the owner, just the car itself. Nondescript, no vanity plates that I could make out, the only visible digits on the plate at all a 5, a 7, and a G. I was about to give it up as another dead end when something dangling from the rearview mirror of the car in picture number one caught my eye.

I leaned over, squinting at the screen. It was fuzzy, tiny, and not the best-quality photo to begin with. But as I tilted my head and leaned back, it took shape. A heart. A shimmery purple heart dangling on a silver chain.

I sucked in a breath.

I knew that heart. I'd seen it before a dozen times. And I knew who it belonged to.

Suddenly everything fit, all the random bits of information that had been floating around in my head falling into a perfect pattern. A perfectly sinister pattern, I realized with a shiver, as I now knew exactly who had killed Courtney. And Kaylee. And who had framed Josh to take the fall for everything.

I switched screens and quickly pulled up Chase's

number, my hands shaking.

"Hey," he answered on the first ring. "You get the pics?"

"Yes! And I know who it is."

"Yeah, the sedan."

"No, I know who owns it."

"Really?" he asked. I could feel him leaning forward, body as tense as mine was, rigid with tension. "Who?"

I opened my mouth to tell him.

But instead of a name, a strangled sort of sound came out.

Probably because something had just been looped around my neck. And pulled tight.

Very tight.

TWENTY-TWO

I DROPPED MY PHONE, BARELY COGNIZANT OF THE CLATTER it made, my hands immediately going to my neck. I clawed at the strap, feeling its rough edges dig into my skin. I tried to suck in air, but it was a no-go. The strap was tight enough to cut off my windpipe, crushing against my throat. Instinctually, I thrashed right, then left, my body fighting all on its own against the lack of oxygen. Unfortunately, whoever was holding the strap behind me was wicked strong and thrashed right along with me, never letting the line go slack enough for me to take a breath.

I felt my vision blurring. My lungs were on fire, and the world was getting smaller and smaller, my vision narrowing in on all sides, like a movie slowly fading to black. My limbs felt heavy, my head heavy. My eyelids so heavy they were threatening to close. I was on borrowed time.

I summoned up all the strength I had left and, fighting against every instinct, let my limbs go slack. Which had exactly the effect I'd hoped. My attacker let up on the reins, the fabric around my neck loosening just a fraction of an inch. That was all I needed.

I jerked forward, then sharply back, my head connecting with my attacker's face.

I heard a soft grunt. Then, "My nose!"

My attacker let go of the strap, and I quickly slipped a hand between it and my bruised neck and slid it over my head. I took one quick step forward, preparing to bolt as fast as I could.

But one step was as far as I got.

I might have stunned my attacker with that head butt, but the recovery was quick. Before I could make my break, I felt an explosion behind my right ear, pain like a white light hammering through my head.

I stumbled forward, my knees hitting the ground, my hands going out to break my fall. I felt skin scraping off my palms as the world rushed up to meet me. Something warm and wet trickled down the side of my face.

"Hartley? You still there?" I heard Chase call from my phone somewhere in the bushes to my right.

But that was the last thing I heard. Just as I reached out to find my cell, pain exploded again. I only had a second to register it before everything went black.

* * *

I blinked my eyes. Ouch. That hurt. I stopped blinking, instead slowly letting my fogged brain come awake. I wasn't sure how long I'd been out, but it felt like a year, every muscle in my body tight and rusty like the Tin Man left out in the rain. I tried the moving thing again, slowly opening my eyes. I had no idea where I was. Somewhere dark. That smelled like mold, something metallic, and sweat. I wrinkled my nose against the offending combo. Ouch. That hurt, too.

If you don't count naturally falling asleep, I had only been unconscious once before. It was when I was ten and had needed a stubborn baby tooth pulled to make room for its overeager adult counterpart. I'd been put under anesthesia, told to count backward from ten and think relaxing thoughts. I'd gotten to three before the world had gone suddenly and completely black. Waking up again after the procedure had been totally disorienting. Like struggling out of a deep sleep, but not even really sure you weren't still dreaming. Like trying to lift yourself out from under a cloudy blanket.

This was kind of like that . . . but with a headache that seemed to extend all the way to the ends of my hair. My head throbbed like someone was playing hip-hop at top volume inside it, and my mouth was dry like I'd been sucking on Sour Patch Kids all night. I moved my tongue around, licking my lips.

Or, more accurately, tried to lick them. Turns out something was stuck over my mouth. If I had to guess, I'd say from the rubbery taste that it was duct tape. Alarm bells clanged in my head as I remembered my last few minutes; the struggle and the fact that I had lost. I wiggled my hands and feet, a bad feeling brewing in my stomach. Yep. They were duct taped as well.

Not good.

I forced myself to blink through the darkness for a glimpse of my attacker, even though each movement of my eyelids felt like an effort of monumental proportions.

Finally objects started to come into view in the shadows. A bassoon. A music stand. A pair of drums in the corner.

The band room.

I had a moment of absolute squick when I saw the woodwind cabinet behind which my boyfr—*ex*-boyfriend— had bopped the chastity queen, but it was overshadowed by the fact that I was bound and gagged. It was never a good sign to find yourself like that.

And an even worse sign?

The door to the band room was slowly opening, a shadow entering. I squinted through the dark to make it out just as the overhead fluorescents switched on, flooding the room with light.

I blinked, trying to ignore the flash of pain that slammed through my head as my pupils dilated. Instead, I focused on the image of my attacker, in the flesh, clearly illuminated in the doorway.

I took a very small comfort in the fact that I had been right about the sedan owner as she grinned at me, showing what $5,000 of orthodontia had paid for.

"Well, good morning, Sleeping Beauty," Caitlyn Calvin said, sarcasm dripping from her voice almost as sickeningly sweet as the purple heart-shaped beads that hung from the ends of her braided hair. "I was wondering when you'd wake up."

"Hmph frphm bemphr."

"What's that?" she asked, taking a step forward.

"HMPH FRPHM BEMPHR!"

She reached a hand out and, in one swift movement, ripped the tape off my mouth.

"Holy hell!" I yelled, feeling at least three layers of skin go with the tape. I bit down hard to stop the stinging.

"Watch your language," Caitlyn chided, making a tsking sound through her teeth.

"Interesting advice coming from a *killer*," I countered.

She narrowed her eyes at me for a second. Then she smiled. A big, scary, sick smile. It was the single creepiest thing I had ever seen outside of a horror movie. How I could have missed the evil lurking just below the surface of her perkatude, I didn't know.

"*Killer* is such an ugly word," she said, scrunching up her ski-jump nose (which, I was happy to see, was swelling as we spoke).

"Killing people is ugly work."

"I prefer to think of it as exacting justice. I'm striking down the unworthy."

"Unworthy of what?"

"Life. Those who are immoral must be punished. And it's my duty to do so."

'Kay, I'd always known there was something slightly off about the Color Guard girls, but I'd never realized just how positively unhinged this chick was until now. I wondered if Courtney had known . . .

"How was killing your best friend your duty?" I asked. Not that I was really interested in the inner workings of Crazy Chick's mind, but generally when a killer knocks someone over the head, ties her up, and begins to confess, it doesn't bode well for the health of the tie-ee. You don't have to be a *CSI* devotee to know that most criminals don't confess when they expect the other person to live through the ordeal.

All things considered, the longer I could keep Caitlyn talking, the better chance I had of coming up with a brilliant plan to get away.

Okay, brain, no time like the present to get brillianting.

Caitlyn twirled one braid in her hands, looking every bit the adorable model student. "Courtney was *president* of the Chastity Club," she explained. "We all looked up to her as our moral compass to guide us thorough the tempting waters of high school."

I couldn't help rolling my eyes. "She was sleeping with my boyfriend."

"I know!" Caitlyn shouted. "It was disgusting. She was making a mockery of everything we stood for."

"So you killed her?"

Caitlyn paused for a moment, then nodded very slowly, a sparkle hitting her eyes that made me wonder if she hadn't enjoyed it.

"I had to, don't you see? If word got out that Courtney Cline was sleeping with someone out of wedlock, no one would take the chastity pledge seriously anymore. Who knows what kind of chaos that would cause?"

Teenagers having sex. Imagine that.

I decided that open sarcasm probably wasn't the best tactic. Instead, I said, "But she was your best friend."

"*Was.* I could never be friends with a hypocrite."

"So what did you do?"

"As soon as Kaylee and I heard the rumors about her and Josh, we decided to stage an intervention. What she was doing with Josh had to be stopped."

"So you tricked her into meeting you at Josh's house?"

She nodded. "We wanted to confront her at the scene of her crimes. Well, *one* scene of her crimes," she said, looking around the band room and wrinkling her nose.

My feelings exactly.

"Anyway, when we were all out on the field for Color Guard practice, Kaylee played lookout while I slipped Josh's phone from his bag and sent the text. Ten minutes later Courtney was begging me for a ride to Josh's place. She fed me some line about needing to see his trig notes, but we knew why she really wanted to see him. We followed her in, and that's when we confronted her about her wicked ways."

"What happened?"

Caitlyn shook her head. "Instead of denying it or being repentant, she flaunted it. How everyone thought she was so chaste and here she was sneaking around with Josh. She was actually proud of the fact that she had the whole school fooled."

Me included.

"And then," Caitlyn went on, "she told us it wasn't the first time. She'd done this before! With boys from other schools!"

"Slut!" I couldn't help it; it just slipped out.

"I know, right?" Caitlyn agreed. "Kaylee and I told her she had to stop. Now! She had to repent, to make amends, to make sure no one at Herbert Hoover High ever found out about the secret immoral life she'd been leading."

"And did she?" I asked, even though the fact that she was dead in my ex-boyfriend's closet kinda answered that one for me. But I needed more time. My eyes scanned the room for something sharp enough to cut my bonds. Bassoon, snare drum, majorette baton. Why was everything here so round and child safe?

"No," Caitlyn answered me. "She did not. You know what she did?"

I shook my head. "What?"

"She laughed. She *laughed* at us! *Us!* Called us prudes. Said we were ridiculous for actually believing that chastity crap. She said she was only doing it to look good on her college app."

"I bet that pissed you off," I said, my eyes still scanning the room.

"Yes. Yes, it did. I realized then that Courtney had to be stopped before she destroyed everything we stood for."

"So you killed her." I spied a metal music stand in the corner, tipped over on its side, the feet sticking up. One of them was a little jagged, like it had seen better days. It looked perfect for sawing through a length of duct tape. If I could just get close enough, I might be able to slide my wrist across its edge. I slowly wriggled backward, eyes on Caitlyn as she spoke.

"I didn't want to kill her. I tried to reason with her. But

she wouldn't listen. Don't you see? It was the only way to stop her. She wasn't going to do it on her own."

"What about Kaylee? Did she agree it was the only way to stop Courtney?"

Caitlyn shrugged. "She thought we should just scare Courtney, that we were just there to put her back on the path to virtue. But I knew better. After Courtney confessed, I knew she was evil and would never change her ways."

"So you strangled her?"

Caitlyn nodded. "It was so easy, really. Courtney had her iPod in her pocket. Kaylee held her down while I grabbed the earbuds and wrapped the wire around her neck. And squeezed."

"Until she stopped breathing." I felt my stomach lurch, imagining Courtney's last moments. My eyes flickered to the fabric strap of Caitlyn's backpack, hanging on her shoulder now, and my imagination didn't have to work too hard, having experienced the same thing just moments (hours? I still wasn't sure how long I'd been tied up in here.) ago. It was not pleasant. Not the way I would wish anyone to spend her last moment on earth, even someone like Courtney Cline.

She nodded. "She struggled a little at first, but it didn't take long before she was still. It was actually a lot easier than I thought. You'd be amazed how fragile life really is."

I hoped I didn't get the opportunity to learn firsthand.

"And Kaylee went along with it?"

"Courtney was dead before she even knew what happened. At that point, she had no choice. She had to go along with it. We stuffed her in the closet and left. I figured Josh would find her later, and everyone would think he did it." She paused. "Dumb luck that you broke in."

"That's me. Miss Dumb Luck."

She ignored me, plowing ahead. "Anyway, it worked out okay. The police thought Josh had killed her and had taken off. Everyone did." She paused, narrowing her eyes at me. "Except you."

Uh-oh. "Sorry?" I squeaked out.

"You just had to butt in. Had to start stirring up doubt, dragging Courtney's character through the mud."

I refrained from pointing out that she had gotten it pretty muddy on her own. Instead, I did my best to deflect the topic of conversation away from my bound and defenseless self.

"I don't understand," I said, scooching backward again. Just a few more inches and I'd be in range of the jagged music stand. "If Kaylee was in on it with you, why kill her?"

For the first time Caitlyn looked almost remorseful. "I didn't want to. Kaylee was good. She was the real deal, a chaste virgin who lived the creed."

"So what happened?" I reached back behind me as far as I could stretch and felt the tips of my fingers come up against the serrated edge. I scooted back just a little more, positioning my wrists until I felt the edge come in contact with tape. Yes!

"What happened was you," she said, sending me an accusing glare.

I froze, the tape stuck on the jagged music stand foot. "Me?"

"Yes, you. You kept asking questions, digging in where you didn't belong. I tried to reassure Kaylee that our plan was foolproof, but the more you nosed around, the more nervous she got. And then she started to question whether we had done the right thing. She was scared and wanted to go to the police. She wanted to confess everything." She shook her head. "What a waste. And it's all your fault!"

"*My* fault? *You* killed her."

"Why did you have to be so nosy? What did you care, anyway? I mean, what did you care if Josh went to jail? The guy cheated on you."

"Yes, I'm aware, thanks." Geez, did everyone have to keep pointing that out? "So, you killed Kaylee?"

She nodded, slowly. "I had to," she repeated. "I overheard you saying that you were meeting a witness at night on the football field. It seemed like the perfect opportunity to take care of both of you. Kaylee needed to be shut up, and if you were the one to find the body, well, I thought maybe it would scare you off. Make you quit poking your nose where it didn't belong."

"Uh-huh." I rubbed the tape at my wrists against the edge, feeling it slowly bite into the tape. Not exactly an instant escape, but if I kept rubbing . . . "Go on," I prompted.

"Well," Caitlyn continued, "I told Kaylee to meet me out there at quarter to midnight. I told her I agreed that we had to go to the police, but we needed to get our stories straight first. That we'd confess to you, and go straight to the police afterward. Poor thing totally believed me." She shook her head as if she really did feel sorry for Kaylee. "She never even saw it coming. I snuck up behind her, whacked her over the head with a rock, and down she went. Quick and painless."

Yeah, except for the whole being-dead part.

"And you left her there as a threat to me?"

She nodded. "I hoped it would scare some sense into you, and you'd mind your own business."

"But I didn't."

She glared at me. "No, you didn't. You asked too many questions. And sooner or later you were going to ask the right one of the right person. And that's why you have to die, too."

Even though I'd been pretty sure she wasn't just going to let me go, hearing her say the words out loud sent a chill up my spine.

"I'm not the only one who knows it was you," I said, hoping I could convince her that the secret didn't die with me.

"Oh really?" she put her hands on her hips.

"Chase saw your car in the photos. He knows it was parked on Josh's street the day of the murder."

She shrugged. "A car on the street is hardly proof that I killed anyone. Lots of people were parked there that day. Josh. You. Chase."

Good point. "And Andi Brackenridge has video of you. She was going to show it to me tonight."

She grinned, showing off all five hundred of her teeth again.

And I felt the pieces click into place once more. "Andi doesn't have video, does she?"

Caitlyn shook her head very slowly.

"And she didn't send me that text today, did she?"

Again with the head shake.

"You did."

She nodded.

"So that you could trap me, strangle me, knock me over the head, and tie me up."

"Actually, I had only planned on strangling you. But

the best laid plans . . ." She shrugged. "I had to improvise a little."

"What about the hoodie?" I asked, doing anything I could to stall her. I rubbed furiously behind my back, almost not even caring if she saw me now. I could feel the tape ripping, the fabric becoming thinner and thinner. If I could just keep her talking a little bit longer . . . "Shiloh Jackson said she saw Chase's black hoodie with a purple eagle on it in the window of Josh's bedroom right before Courtney was killed."

She cocked her head. "You mean *my* black hoodie with a purple *butterfly* on it?"

Mental face palm. So Shiloh hadn't been lying; she'd just seen what she wanted to see in that window. I suddenly felt so stupid for having doubted Chase. If I ever got out of here, I was going to spend the rest of high school making it up to him.

If.

"So, what are you going to do now?" I asked. Even though a sneak preview of my own death wasn't exactly my idea of a good time, I needed a few more seconds before I could get my hands free.

"Now, there's going to be a terrible accident," Caitlyn said, looking as if she almost believed her own story. "There's going to be a fire. In the band room. With the ancient wiring in these rickety old portables, it was bound to happen sometime. And, as they clear the wreckage, they'll find a body among the ruins."

Sweat traveled down my spine. "Mine?" I asked.

She nodded. "Horrible tragedy that you just happened to be investigating in the band room when it went up in flames." She pulled a lighter out of her backpack. "Fire is the perfect way to cover evidence. Especially once the firefighters blast their hoses all over the scene."

"You'll never get away with it," I said, realizing I sounded frighteningly like a character in a *Scooby-Doo* episode.

She shrugged. "Josh is in custody. You're about to die. I already have gotten away with it."

She had a point.

And, I noticed as she reached into her purse, she also had a can of lighter fluid.

I watched in horror as she uncapped the can and poured the acrid liquid on the floor. With slow, methodical movements, she started to walk around the room, liberally dosing the area by the door, then spraying the wooden instrument cabinets.

"You're really serious?" I asked, feeling adrenaline build up in my chest as she created a path of lighter fluid that led right to me.

She looked hurt. "Of course I'm serious. Why doesn't anyone ever take Color Guard girls seriously?"

That was a loaded question I was way too preoccupied to properly answer at the moment.

"You can't do this," I sputtered.

"I already am."

"Your plan is flawed," I said, desperately buying time.

She paused. Cocked her head. "How so?"

"There is one thing you didn't count on," I said, feeling the last of my bonds finally give way.

She scrunched up her adorable little swollen nose. "What?"

"A broken music stand," I said.

A wrinkle nestled between her eyebrows. "A what?"

I took her moment of confusion to act. It was now or never. I took a deep breath, then launched myself forward, tearing my hands apart with a loud rip as the last of the duct tape gave way.

I tackled her from the front, knocking her back onto her butt, the can flying from her hand to hit the far wall.

"Uhn." Caitlyn's head hit the floor, smacking loudly against the linoleum.

But she wasn't dazed for long. She reached both hands up and grabbed a handful of my hair, tugging.

I screamed, my head following where she tugged, flipping me off her and down onto the floor beside her. I reached out, smacking indiscriminately in the direction of her face. I felt a couple slaps connect, but it didn't loosen her grip on my hair any.

"Let. Go," I said through gritted teeth, my scalp on fire.

"Stop hitting me," she responded, ducking as I connected with her cheek.

No way. I was fighting for dear life. If I lost, I was toast. Literally, if Caitlyn had her way.

We both tugged, slapped, and punched, hoping the other one would say "uncle." And I felt myself losing the upper hand my momentary element of surprise had gained. Apparently carrying those tall flags around had made Caitlyn's arms crazy strong. She was winning.

I struggled against her, kicking with my legs. One foot connected with the rack of clarinets, sending a spray of wind instruments raining down on us. One thunked me in the head, knocking my headache into migraine territory.

A couple hit Caitlyn on the shoulder, causing her to lose her grip and roll to the right.

"My hair beads!" she screamed, as little purple hearts scattered across the floor. "That's it—now you're going to pay."

Uh-oh.

Caitlyn lunged forward and grabbed my upper arm, dragging me to my feet and slamming me into the back wall.

I felt my teeth rattle as the jolt echoed through my

body. It stunned me for a moment, but I quickly recovered, diving forward toward her.

Unfortunately, as I lunged at Caitlyn, I also knocked into a rack of French horns. They came tumbling down, hitting a tuba propped up against the wall beside the rack, and clattering to the floor.

And, even more horrible, creating a spark.

I watched in horror as the spark hit a puddle of lighter fluid on the floor, instantly erupting it into a live flame. Which spread like a dynamite line across the back wall, down the center of the room, through the woodwind section, and into a pile of sheet music that instantly went up in flames, throwing Bach, Beethoven, and Sousa around the room in a whoosh of glowing flames.

I blinked.

So not good.

Caitlyn jumped back from the flaming sheet music. I could see her mental wheels turning. Not exactly as she had planned, but improvisation seemed to be working for her. Especially since she was on the side of the room nearest the door and I was on the side nearest a growing wall of fire.

Caitlyn looked from me to the door. She shrugged. "Sorry, Hartley," she said.

And before I could even protest, Caitlyn had slipped out the door to freedom.

And I was alone. In a flaming band room. With the exit blocked.

Miss Dumb Luck strikes again.

My head whipped around wildly, looking for any possible escape route. Windows? Not allowed in portables. Cracks in the walls? I scooted as far back into the only gasless corner that I could, feeling the heat from the flames creating a sunburn effect on my cheeks. I was slowly roasting like a pig. I pushed on the walls. Solid. No cracks, no holes, no way to get out.

And the flames were growing, backing me into a corner.

I fought down the urge to cry like a baby, instead feeling my way along the wall for any possible place to hide from the inferno intent on roasting me alive. My fingers explored the wall behind me as I slunk to the left, one eye on the flames. Unfortunately, the only thing they came upon was a pile of pom-poms stacked in the corner. For lack of a better plan, I grabbed one and threw it into the fire licking at my feet. It made a sizzling sound, turning the flames to blue and purple, setting off a noxious smell. But it slowed their progress toward me.

I quickly grabbed another pom-pom and tossed it. It wasn't putting the fire out, but it was buying me time.

"Help!" I screamed, my voice quickly gobbled up by the crackling flames. "Help me! I'm in here!" I yelled again. Not that I had much hope of anyone hearing me. I'd seen for myself just how deserted the campus was. But I was out of other options.

"Heeeeeeeelp!" I yelled again, throwing another pom-pom onto the fire.

My voice was hoarse by the time I got down to the last pom-pom, and my skin was turning a bright red. Flames pushed closer, showing no sign of mercy.

This was it. The end of the road. I never thought this was the way I would go. Honestly, I never put much thought into going at all. Going was something old people did. Not sixteen-year-olds. Only here I was. Sixteen, and going like a marshmallow at a campfire.

Those tears got the better of me, sliding silently down my cheeks as I thought of Mom. She was going to be so pissed when she found out I'd snuck out to my death. I pictured Raley giving her the news, his fatherly face drawn in concern. I pictured Sam when she heard about her best friend being barbecued. What would she say? What about the other students at HHH? Would Ms. Bessie be overrun with the grief stricken, or would they spend a day wearing designer armbands, then go about their business as if I'd never existed?

And what about Chase?

Funny that I would think of him at a time like this. I'd only just met him—it wasn't like he had played a big role in my life.

But I did. I thought of him and the regret I felt for thinking he could be a killer. For the hurt I'd seen in his eyes that day. For rummaging through his room. For not letting him finish his striptease before I popped out from under his bed.

In fact, I was thinking so much of Chase, that I almost thought I saw him. I was clearly hallucinating, the toxic fumes from the melting pom-poms finally hitting my brain. I hallucinated his shape through the haze of smoke choking the room: the flames licking at the corners of my vision as I watched my hallucination leap over a pile of burning clarinets, his form covered in a wet cape, hands reaching through the last of the flaming pom-poms toward me.

Then they grabbed me around the shoulders.

Wow, this was one strong hallucination.

"Hartley!" he yelled at me.

I blinked through the smoke and my own hazy brain. "Chase?"

"Hold on to me."

I did, grabbing the wet hand that reached out toward me.

A second later the wet cloak was around my shoulders, too, and Chase was dragging me back through the flames out toward the door. A second later, the heat of the flaming room gave way to a slap of cold air on my cheeks, the wet cloak falling to the ground. Me with it.

"Hart? Hartley, talk to me. Are you okay?" Chase

said, leaning over me.

I looked up into his face. I put a hand out and touched the fine stubble on his cheek. What do you know—he was actually real.

"Say something," he choked out, his eyebrows drawn into a tight line.

"Something."

He let out a sound that might have been a sigh or a sob, I wasn't quite sure. He reached down and hugged me to him even more fiercely than Mom ever had.

Then he did something totally unexpected, which made me once again wonder if I was hallucinating.

He kissed me.

His lips covered mine softly and slowly, tasting like coffee and peppermint gum.

I experienced one full second of heaven.

Then I promptly passed out.

TWENTY-THREE

I WOKE UP, LYING ON A STRETCHER. NOT THAT I COULD SEE it, but from my vantage point—staring up at the dark sky, an EMT taking my blood pressure and my head strapped to a rigid wooden board—I surmised I was on a stretcher. Brilliant, no?

After answering a few routine questions like what my name was, what day it was (which was a hazy one because I wasn't sure how much time had elapsed between my midnight meet and now), and who the president was, I was deemed okay. At least okay enough to get unstrapped from the wooden board.

That was about when Mom arrived, grabbing me in a hug that didn't end. Seriously, I think we stood there for a full five minutes before she finally let me go, tears in her eyes. Which of course caused tears to well up in my eyes. Which led to the two of us becoming blubbering messes of *I love you*s (mostly from her) and *I'll never sneak out again*s (mostly from me) by the time Detective Raley walked up with his little black notebook in hand.

I blame the blubbering for the fact that it took another ten minutes before I was finally able to get the full story out for Raley.

"So, Caitlyn was the one who sent you the text to meet her here?" he asked, consulting his notes.

I nodded. (Which, by the way did not feel good. My fight with Caitlyn, coupled with inhaling mass amounts of pom-pom smoke, had caused that migraine to grow to monstrous proportions.) "And she strangled Courtney and hit Kaylee on the back of the head with a rock."

He raised an eyebrow. "And she told you all this?"

I moved to nod again but thankfully thought better of it just in time. "Yes. Right before she tried to barbecue me."

"Uh-huh."

"Look, I know this sounds kinda crazy, but you have to believe me, Caitlyn was—"

But he cut me off with an "I do."

I paused. "You do what?"

"Believe you."

I clamped my mouth shut with a click. "Oh."

"Chase called us as soon as he pulled you out of the building."

Bad Boy had the cops on speed dial? Who knew.

Apparently, according to Raley's notebook, Chase had been concerned when I'd dropped my phone, and he promptly got into his death trap, racing through the streets toward the school (one time I was grateful for his maniac driving skills). He'd searched the football field for me and was just about to give up and call Raley to report me missing when he'd seen flames rising from the band room. Thinking quickly, he'd soaked a blanket he had in the back of his car with water from the pool and wrapped himself in it to burst in and rescue me.

Very action hero. Very hot. (Hey, after the night I'd had, I think I earned the right to pull one bad pun or two.)

He had taken off, by the way. By the time I came to, Chase was nowhere to be seen, making me wonder if my mind had, in fact, been playing tricks on me with The Kiss. I licked my lips. I was almost sure I could taste him there.

"We have an APB out on Caitlyn," Raley continued, "and a uniformed officer is on his way to her house right now. We'll pick her up, don't worry."

And for the first time in days, I actually didn't.

"And in the meantime?" Mom asked. "Should we hide Hartley? Should we leave town? Should we put her in some sort of protective custody?"

Raley looked at me. Then nodded toward Mom and

rolled his eyes, a half smile playing on the corner of his lips.

I couldn't help returning it.

"I'm fine, Mom," I told her.

Mom looked at me. "You have no eyebrows. You are not fine."

My hands flew to my eyebrows. Or, more accurately, the bald skin where they used to be.

Noooooooooo!

"They'll grow back," Raley assured me. "And in the meantime, I think you're perfectly safe to return home. We have the situation under control. I'll let you know as soon as we have Caitlyn in custody."

Mom was still not totally convinced, but when I begged her to go home and whip me up a plate of soy cheesecake with gluten-free walnut crust, she relented, piling me into the minivan.

It was nearing dawn by the time we arrived. I was beyond exhausted. But, instead of collapsing onto my bed, I followed Mom to the kitchen.

"So," she asked tentatively as she grabbed a mixing bowl from the top shelf, "you feel like talking, hon? I mean, if you don't, that's fine. I understand."

But honestly? I did.

So, I did.

As Mom mixed tofu, fructose, and soy milk, I told her

everything that had happened in the past week, ever since I stumbled upon Courtney in Josh's closet. I hesitated a few times, waiting for the SMother to pounce, but, amazingly, she didn't. At least, not until I hit the end.

When she rounded the kitchen counter and gave me another five-minute hug.

"Don't ever scare me like that again," she mumbled into my hair.

Don't worry. I had no intention of ever getting involved with something like this again.

Detective Raley caught up with Caitlyn the next morning. She had stayed on the run all night, but skipping school was too much for a good Color Guard girl to do, even a killer. She was arrested the second she tried to enter school grounds and was heard yelling about her trig homework as she was dragged away in handcuffs. The KTVU news reported that she was looking at an insanity plea—saying that the pressure of high school perfection made her do it. Creative, I'd give her that. Rumor had it she was being held in a psychiatric facility, where she was busy converting the mentally unstable into born-again virgins.

With Caitlyn in custody, Josh was released and all charges were dropped. He returned to school the following Monday, and, for the first time in two weeks, all eyes were on him, the whispers and stares directed at someone else for a change. Part of me felt kinda sorry for him. I mean, he had been framed, arrested, and locked up in jail—not something I'd wish on anyone.

But as much as he'd been my first love, he'd also been the first guy to ever cheat on me. And if I'd learned anything from my near-barbecuing experience, it was that life was way too short to spend with someone who didn't respect me. I had run a murder investigation. I had figured out the killer even when the police couldn't. I had survived being attacked and brought a murderer to justice. I was awesome, and I deserved so much better.

So I let Josh suffer the stares and whispers on his own.

Kaylee's funeral was that Wednesday, but I didn't attend. Her parents specified family and close friends only, and I didn't think I qualified as either. Even though I knew she had played a role in Courtney's death, I still kinda felt sorry for Kaylee. It was clear she hadn't realized what Caitlyn was doing until it was too late. And, in the end, she had tried to do the right thing. So I wore a black armband shot through with purple sparkly threads in her honor that day.

Courtney's funeral, on the other hand, was so well attended they ended up using the football stadium to hold everyone and had to set up three extra banks of Porta Potties in the parking lot. Guys from all the area high schools showed up and even some college guys from San

José State. Apparently the chastity queen really had gotten around.

And that fact was exploited to the fullest on Shiloh's blog. She got so many hits to The Mainstream Sucks after the fire and Caitlyn's arrest that she started charging for sidebar advertising space. A chance several businesses jumped at. Instead of her brother's old ten-speed, Shiloh was soon seen driving a brand-new convertible BMW to school. (Yeah, I was seriously thinking of taking up blogging now.)

The local news station ran an entire series of stories on the HHH Killer. After Andi Brackenridge's blackmail attempt came out in the news, Mary May fired her for unladylike conduct. Andi then hired a kick-butt civil attorney, who sued for unlawful termination. Rumor had it, Andi was looking at a settlement that would cover the cost of raising her little pink bundle. Several times over.

Of course, while the local news stations grabbed the story with gusto, the *Herbert Hoover High Homepage* had been the first news outlet to publish the entire string of events, Chase getting his promised exclusive. In fact, his article was actually reprinted in both the *Weekly Times* and the *San José Mercury News* with his byline, giving him just the kind of clipping that would get him into the journalism school of his choice next year.

Not that I had firsthand knowledge of his choice. In fact, ever since The Kiss, we hadn't spoken. Which I guess

I shouldn't have been surprised about. I mean, now that the whole case was over, and he had his story, we really didn't have any reason to hang out together. We lived in different worlds. Ran in different circles. Our tentative partnership was over.

Which was fine. I was so over men in general, and the ones at our school specifically. Josh, Chase, and the whole childish bunch of them could go take a flying leap for all I cared. Which is exactly what I told Sam that afternoon over meat(ish) loaf in the cafeteria.

"I honestly don't even care that he hasn't spoken to me since we came back to school," I told her.

"Who, Josh?"

"Chase."

She raised an eyebrow, then sipped from her juice box.

"What? What's with the eyebrow?"

"Nothing."

"Don't nothing me, Samantha Kramer. What?"

"It's just . . ."

"What?"

She grinned. "You've said his name six times."

I paused. "No. I don't think so."

She nodded, her bangs bobbing against her forehead. "Yup. I counted. While telling me how much you don't care about men, you've said the name 'Chase' six times."

I bit my lip. "So?"

She shrugged. Then sipped her juice box again. "That's

a lot of times, that's all."

"So what. So I said his name six times. I say lots of things lots of times."

"Uh-huh."

"It doesn't mean anything."

"Uh-huh."

"Besides, weren't you listening? I am over guys. Guys suck. They bring nothing but trouble. This whole thing started because of a suckish guy. God, if I could just go back in time and not date Josh, I'd still have eyebrows."

"They'll grow back."

"That's what everyone keeps saying," I mumbled, self-consciously fingering the still-bald patch above my right eye where I'd tried to draw an eyebrow with an eyeliner pencil. Which, by the way blended perfectly with the bright red burn on my face that made me look like I'd fallen asleep on a tanning bed. And the purple bruise around my neck that was just now starting to fade. And the lump at my temple where Caitlyn had hit me was a lovely shade of baby poop brown now. Yep, I was a regular prize.

"Well, don't look now," Sam said, glancing over my shoulder, "but here he comes."

"Josh?" I asked, ducking and grabbing my tray, ready to make a hasty exit.

She shook her head. "No, Chase."

I bit my lip.

"Oh."

I did an eeny, meeny, miny, moe whether or not I had time to bolt for an exit before he saw me. Not that I had any reason to bolt. I had done nothing wrong. So we'd kissed. So what? Big deal. People kissed all the time. It didn't mean anything. It had happened in the heat of the moment. (Ugh. There went a pun again.) I was emotional, hallucinating. He'd just rescued me from a burning building. Anything that happened afterward didn't count. Everyone knew that.

Apparently I took so long convincing myself I didn't need to flee that Chase's tray plopped down on the Formica table beside me before I had a chance to *not* act on the instinct.

"Hey," he said, straddling the bench next to me.

Close next to me.

My cheeks instantly heated, awkward butterflies floating around in my stomach.

"Hey," I managed, covering my blush with my hair.

"Hey, Sam."

"Hey."

"Hey," I repeated.

"You already said that," he pointed out.

"Oh."

Sam looked from Chase to me. Then back at Chase.

"Okay, well, I've got to go . . . you know, so, I'll catch

you later, yeah?" she said, gathering her juice box and paper bag.

I opened my mouth to beg her to stay, but she was already skittering away, backpack on one shoulder. She did a "call me" sign over her shoulder.

Great. Alone with Bad Boy.

"So . . ." he said, ripping open his ranch dipping sauce.

"So."

"Your eyebrows look good," he said, gesturing to my eyeliner job.

I ducked my face back down behind my hair again. "Thanks. They should grow back soon."

He nodded. "Cool. Look, there's something I wanted to talk to you about, Hartley."

"It didn't mean anything," I blurted out. Then immediately wished I was one of those girls who knew how to keep her mouth shut in an awkward situation.

The thing was, I was totally afraid to hear what Chase had to say. As much as I was secure in my newfound awesomeness, the whole Josh thing was still raw. At least for now. Maybe in a few days, weeks, months, when my eyebrows grew back and my pride had a chance to grow back along with them, I'd be a little less chicken around the opposite sex. But for now? *Bawk, bawk, ba-gawk!*

"Didn't mean anything?" Chase asked, cocking his head.

I licked my lips. "Yeah. I mean, I was vulnerable, you

know? I was out of it. From the smoke. And the fire. And the pom-pom fumes. I thought maybe I was hallucinating you at first. And you rescued me, so I was all like 'my hero' and stuff and it was just the hea—" I stopped myself just in time from punning this up. "It was the moment, ya know? So, I totally know that it doesn't mean anything. I'm totally not reading anything into it that isn't really there. I know that Shiloh is your type, like the dark and weird and dangerous girls, and I'm like vanilla with tofu, so I know it was a mistake and just a fluke and that it totally didn't mean anything, so you don't have to 'talk,'" I said doing Raley-style air quotes, "to me about it, because we're cool, okay?"

I paused for a breath.

And looked up to find Chase doing a lopsided smile at me.

"What on earth are you talking about?" he said.

I bit my lip. "The Kiss?"

Something momentarily flickered behind his eyes, but just as quickly it disappeared. "That's not what I wanted to talk to you about."

Mental face palm.

"Oh. Right. Well, okay, then."

He grinned even bigger, showing off a row of teeth. "You're blushing."

"It's the fire burn."

"It's cute."

"Did you want something?" I asked, blushing so hard I

feared my cheeks would turn purple.

"Yes, I did," he said, popping a pizza stick in his mouth as if nothing in the world could ever make him feel embarrassed or awkward—especially not a kiss that meant so little he didn't even know what I was talking about. "I thought we worked well together on the story."

I raised an eyebrow (or a place where an eyebrow would be) his way. "You did?"

"You know, when you weren't accusing me of being a killer."

"Yeah. Sorry about that."

He waved it off. "Anyway, I wanted to know if you wanted a spot on the paper. The *Homepage* could use a reporter like you."

"Like me?"

"Smart, tenacious, resourceful." He paused, then grinned at me again. "Willing to sacrifice her eyebrows for the truth."

"They're growing back," I repeated.

"So, what do you say? Wanna come work for me?"

I bit the inside of my cheek. Honestly, I'd never had any journalistic aspirations. Writing an essay for English was about as much typing as I wanted to do. On the other hand . . . I had to admit there was a certain satisfaction in digging Caitlyn out of hiding. Sort of like doing a puzzle where the pieces were all in 3-D. And human.

Besides, after all the ditching I'd done lately, I could see my grades slipping. If I wanted to get into a good college, I was going to need some serious extracurricular stuff to pad my applications.

"Okay," I finally said. "I'll do it."

"Cool." He popped another pizza stick in. "Room thirty-five. After school. I'll give you your first assignment today."

"I'll be there."

He downed his last pizza stick and grabbed his tray, unfolding himself from the bench and moving to stand up.

"Oh, and . . . by the way?"

"Yeah?" I asked, looking up at him.

"Shiloh is not my type."

"Oh?" I asked, my voice going an octave higher than play-it-cool-girl would have liked.

He shook his head. "Actually, I've got a thing for blondes."

I gulped down a shiver.

He grinned.

"See ya later, partner," he said, then walked away.

I watched his tall, broad-shouldered form strut through the cafeteria, tossing his tray in the bus line, before exiting the room.

Oh boy.

This was going to be a *very* interesting year.

THE BODY COUNT IS RISING IN

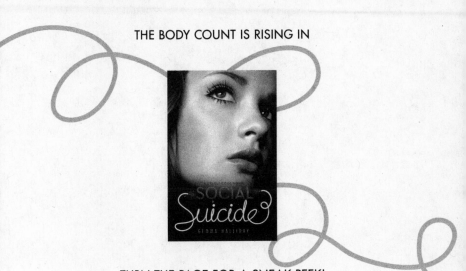

TURN THE PAGE FOR A SNEAK PEEK!

ONE

YOU HAD TO BE INCREDIBLY STUPID TO GET CAUGHT CHEATING in Mr. Tipkins's class, but then again, Sydney Sanders was known for being blonder than Paris Hilton.

HOMECOMING QUEEN HOPEFUL
SUSPENDED FOR CHEATING ON TEST

I looked down at my headline for the *Herbert Hoover High Homepage*, our school's online newspaper. Usually our news ran the exciting gambit from the janitor retiring to a hair being found in the Tuesday Tacos in the cafeteria. So a cheating story was way huge. And I'd been surprised when our paper's editor, Chase Erikson, had assigned me the biggest story since the principal's car was tagged in the back parking lot. After all, I'd only been working on the

Homepage for a short time, making me the resident newbie.

I had a bad feeling that this story was some sort of a test. Do well and I'd earn the respect of my fellow reporters as well as a certain editor with whom I had a complicated personal history. Fail and it was the cafeteria beat for me.

Clearly I was shooting for outcome number one.

I turned up the volume on my iPod in an effort to drown out the noise of the school paper's tiny workroom and put my fingers to the keyboard.

Herbert Hoover High Homecoming Queen nominee Sydney Sanders was discovered cheating on Tuesday's midterm in her precalculus class. Mr. Tipkins caught Sydney red-handed when he noticed the answers to the test painted on her fingernails. Apparently Sydney had incorporated the letters A, B, C, or D into the design painted on her fake nails in the exact order that the answers appeared on Tuesday's test. After Sydney was caught, it quickly came to light that her best friend, Quinn Leslie, had cheated on her test as well. Both girls are suspended from HHH while administrators investigate how the answers to the midterm got out. Sydney, previously considered a front-runner in the upcoming elections, will no longer be eligible to be Herbert Hoover High's Homecoming Queen at next Saturday's dance.

"That the cheating story?" Chase asked, suddenly behind me.

Very close behind me.

I cleared my throat as the scent of fresh soap and fabric softener filled my personal space. I pulled out one earbud and answered, "Yeah. It is."

He was quiet for a moment reading my laptop screen over my shoulder. I felt nerves gathering in my belly as I waited for his reaction.

Chase Erikson was the reason I'd joined the school paper in the first place. He and I had both been investigating a murder at our school, each for different reasons. Chase because he was all about a hot story. And me because the murdered girl had been the president of the Chastity Club and had just happened to be sleeping with my boyfriend. Needless to say, he was now totally an ex-boyfriend. Anyway, Chase and I had sort of teamed up to find the Chastity Club killer, and once we did, Chase told me that I showed promising investigative skills and offered me a position on staff. Considering my college résumé was in need of some padding, I agreed.

So far working on the paper was a lot more fun than I had anticipated. When I'd first heard the term *school paper* I'd envisioned a bunch of extra-credit-hungry geeks with newsprint-stained fingers. But in reality, the entire paper operated online—no newsprint—and several students I knew contributed—none of them geeks. Ashley Stannic did a gossip column once a week that was total LOLs, even if only half the rumors she printed were true. Chris Fret contributed sports commentary and kept a running poll on this semester's favorite player. In fact, the only thing that hadn't been all smiley faces about working at the paper so far was Chase himself.

Chase was tall, broad-shouldered, and built like an athlete. His hair was black, short, and spiky on top, gelled into the perfect tousled style. His eyes were dark and usually twinkling with a look that said he knew a really good secret no one else was in on. He almost always wore black, menacing boots and lots of leather.

One time Mom picked me up from the paper for a dentist appointment and, when she met Chase, described him as "a little rough around the edges." When Ashley Stannic played truth or dare at Jessica Hanson's sweet sixteen and had been pressed to tell the truth, she'd described Chase as "sex in a pair of jeans." Me? I wasn't quite sure what I thought of Chase. All I knew was that things had been uncomfortable and a little awkward between us since The Kiss.

Yes. I, Hartley Grace Featherstone, had swapped spit with HHH's resident Bad Boy.

When we'd worked together on that first story, I'd ended up getting kidnapped and almost killed. Almost, because

Chase had been there to save me at the last minute. And as soon as Chase had rescued me, he'd kissed me.

Briefly. In the heat of the moment. When emotions were running high.

It was a night neither of us had spoken of since, and I was 99 percent sure that it had meant nothing at all beyond relief on both our parts that I was still alive.

But that other 1 percent still persisted just enough that in situations like this—where the scent of his fabric softener was making me lean in so close that I could feel the heat from his body on my cheek—I still wasn't sure whether I thought of Chase as sex in a pair of jeans or a guy who was a little rough around the edges.

"This is good," Chase said, bringing me back to the present.

"Thanks." I felt myself grinning at his praise.

"But you can do better."

And just like that, my grin dropped like a football player's GPA.